A KISS

KING

Barbara Cartland

Barbara Cartland Ebooks Ltd

This edition © 2012

Book design by M-Y Books
m-ybooks.co.uk

The Barbara Cartland
Eternal Collection

The Barbara Cartland Eternal Collection is the unique opportunity to collect all five hundred of the timeless beautiful romantic novels written by the world's most celebrated and enduring romantic author.

Named the Eternal Collection because Barbara's inspiring stories of pure love, just the same as love itself, the books will be published on the internet at the rate of four titles per month until all five hundred are available.

The Eternal Collection, classic pure romance available worldwide for all time .

✳

THE LATE DAME BARBARA CARTLAND

Barbara Cartland, who sadly died in May 2000 at the grand age of ninety eight, remains one of the world's most famous romantic novelists. With worldwide sales of over one billion, her outstanding 723 books have been translated into thirty six different languages, to be enjoyed by readers of romance globally.

Writing her first book 'Jigsaw' at the age of 21, Barbara became an immediate bestseller. Building upon this initial success, she wrote continuously throughout her life, producing bestsellers for an astonishing 76 years. In addition to Barbara Cartland's legion of fans in the UK and across Europe, her books have always been immensely popular in the USA. In 1976 she achieved the unprecedented feat of having books at numbers 1 & 2 in the prestigious B. Dalton Bookseller bestsellers list.

Although she is often referred to as the 'Queen of Romance', Barbara Cartland also wrote several historical biographies, six autobiographies and numerous theatrical plays as well as books on life, love, health and cookery. Becoming one of Britain's most popular media personalities and dressed in her trademark pink, Barbara spoke on radio and television about social and political issues, as well as making many public appearances.

In 1991 she became a Dame of the Order of the British Empire for her contribution to literature and her work for humanitarian and charitable causes.

Known for her glamour, style, and vitality Barbara Cartland became a legend in her own lifetime. Best remembered for her wonderful romantic novels and loved by millions of readers worldwide, her books remain treasured for their heroic heroes, plucky heroines and traditional values. But above all, it was Barbara Cartland's overriding belief in the positive power of love to help, heal and improve the quality of life for everyone that made her truly unique.

Author's Note

Nice and Savoy became part of the French Empire on April 2nd, 1860, a few weeks after this story finishes.

There was a plebiscite but, to the English, it was an act of unjustifiable aggression.

In England the invasion panic did not end suddenly, it gradually faded away. By mid-1861 Britain had increased her ironclads from four to fifteen, and with the new Armstrong reflect guns her Statesmen felt the worst was over.

But relations between Victorian England and Imperial France never fully recovered from the panic years.

In 1870 the French Second Empire suffered an ignominious collapse with the Emperor's defeat by the Prussians at the battle of Sedan.

Although for the sake of the story I have described *H.M.S. Warrior* – Britain's first ironclad – as being in use in 1860, the actual launching took place a year later.

Chapter One 1860

"I love you, Anastasia!"

"I am sorry, Christopher."

"I want to talk to you. Where can we go where we can talk?"

"Nowhere here in the Castle, as you well know."

"There is something I have to tell you."

"Then it will have to wait."

Her Royal Highness Princess Anastasia glanced at her partner mischievously as she spoke, but there was a grim look on Viscount Lyncombe's face as he swung her round the red drawing room in Windsor Castle to a Viennese waltz.

The flickering light from hundreds of candles glinted on the dancing couples and sparkled on the decorations worn by the gentlemen.

The ladies in their crinolines looked like lovely swans and moved with a grace that was almost indescribable. Nevertheless, there had been a slight frown on the Queen's face when, earlier, she had watched her guests dancing the more spirited Mazurka and a German dance called the Gross Vater.

"I have to talk to you, Anastasia," Viscount Lyncombe said insistently. "It concerns you – and you must hear me."

"If you are going to propose to me again, Christopher," Princess Anastasia replied, "there is really no use in my listening. You know it is impossible for us to marry each other."

"Why should it be?" the Viscount asked surlily.

"Because I am Royal – although much good it does me!"

"What does that signify?" he asked. "After all, my father's title is one of the oldest in Great Britain. We were Earls at the time of Agincourt, while your – "

He paused, as if he realised that what he had been about to say would have appeared rude.

"All right, say it!" Princess Anastasia urged.

" – your country has been swallowed up by Prussia."

"Papa may have been a Hohlenstein," Princess Anastasia said, "but Mama is a cousin of the Queen, and you know as well as I do that Her Majesty would never allow any of us to marry a man not of Royal blood."

"We can run away," the Viscount suggested.

He spoke so urgently that the Princess looked at him in surprise.

She had known Christopher Lyncombe ever since she had been a child, because the Countess of Coombe and her mother were close friends.

He was six years older than she was and had teased her, when she was hardly old enough to walk, until she cried. He had pulled her hair and in later years had forced her to 'fag' for him whenever Princess Beatrice, the Grand Duchess of Hohlenstein had stayed with the Earl and Countess of Coombe at their country seat.

It was only now, when Anastasia was nearly eighteen that the Viscount, who had led a very gay and dashing life in London, had fallen in love with her.

~ 4 ~

He himself had been somewhat surprised at the tumultuous emotion she aroused in him, and to Anastasia it was something she had never expected to happen, even in her wildest dreams.

"Are you serious?" she enquired now.

As she spoke she glanced around to be quite certain that no one could hear their conversation.

Fortunately, the Christmas Party at Windsor Castle had been a very large one, and when the Queen had decided to give a ball on the last day of their visit, only a small number of people from outside had been invited to join what was essentially a family occasion.

"Of course I am serious," the Viscount asserted angrily.

"I love you, Anastasia, and I cannot live without you!"

"It is hard for me to believe that you do in fact love me," Anastasia replied. "I have not forgotten how unkind you were to me two years ago, when I was bitten by mosquitoes and you persisted in calling me 'Your Royal Spottiness'!"

"You did not look then as you do now," he answered, his eyes on her small, heart-shaped face which was turned up to his.

Then almost angrily he added,

"You are lovely! You know that, of course! And you are too lovely for me to lose you, Anastasia."

"Why are you talking like this," Anastasia asked, "here, at this moment?"

The Viscount paused for a moment as if he was considering his words, and then he said,

"My father was at the Privy Council this morning. They decided your future!"

"Decided my future?" Anastasia echoed in amazement.

"That is why you have to come away with me. We will go anywhere you like in the world where no one can stop us marrying each other, and where we can be together."

"Where could we go?" Anastasia asked curiously.

"Anywhere you wish," the Viscount replied. "I have plenty of money, and we would be so happy that nothing else would matter."

"The Queen would prevent it – I am sure she would! Anyway, I am not certain I would be happy, ostracised by everyone I have ever known and having to live in some obscure place abroad."

"That is exactly what you are going to have to do!" the Viscount said.

Again Anastasia looked up at him, her blue eyes very wide.

"What have they – decided I have to – do?" she asked, barely above a whisper.

"Marry Maximilian of Maurona!"

"The King?"

"Yes, the King. You will be a Queen, Anastasia, and married to a man you have never seen. Married to a man who, from all I hear, is not at all the right sort of husband for you."

"How do you know – this?" Anastasia asked.

"My father said it was the Queen's suggestion and the British Ambassador has been recalled from Maurona to receive instructions. The alliance has already been proposed to the King."

"He may refuse to – marry me," Anastasia said, almost as if she spoke to herself.

"He will have no choice in the matter, any more than you have," the Viscount retorted. "Maurona is too small a country to defy Great Britain, and although the King would not mind being annexed by the French, the Mauronians themselves would dislike it very much."

"Why should the King not mind?" Anastasia asked curiously.

"Because, if you want the truth," the Viscount replied, "His Majesty is infatuated with everything French, especially their women. When he is not in Paris enjoying himself with all the beauties of the Second Empire, he is having what amounts to a scandalous association with the French Ambassador's wife."

The Viscount spoke spitefully, and then he added in a somewhat shamefaced manner,

"I should not be telling you this, but I want you to realise how impossible it is for you to marry such a man."

"Have you ever met him?" Anastasia enquired.

The Viscount did not reply for a moment as he steered her carefully and in silence past the Queen, who was dancing sedately with one of the Prince Consort's Coburg cousins.

When they were out of earshot, the Viscount replied,

"Yes, I have met him twice. He is pleasant enough, as a man's man, but he is certainly not the right husband for you, Anastasia."

"Have I no – say in the – matter?" Anastasia asked in a rather small voice.

"You know full well you will not even be consulted," Viscount Lyncombe answered. "You will just be told that you are to be married, and let me tell you also that you will not even have time to think about it. It is a question of urgency."

"Why? Explain to me why!" Anastasia begged.

"Because, and here I am giving away secrets," the Viscount replied, "there is a rumour in the Foreign Office that the Emperor, having arranged an Armistice with Austria, and being out for new conquests, is contemplating annexing both Nice and Savoy."

"But surely he cannot do that?" Anastasia asked.

"Why should he not?" Viscount Lyncombe replied. "After all, if the French can consider invading us, a small principality on the Continent is child's play compared with the conquest of Britain."

"I have never believed there was any real danger of that," Anastasia said.

At the same time she did not speak very convincingly.

The tension in England two years before made the Government approve the formation of a Volunteer Rifle Corps as an auxiliary to the Regular Army and Militia. The response had been overwhelming – 134,000 men had enrolled within a few weeks. The Volunteers eagerly left their less exciting jobs to drill twenty-four days a year for their Queen and country in front of their admiring wives and sweethearts.

Village greens and city parks were filled with the fanfare of bugles and skirmishes to teach the art of war. Patriotism and the desire to be ready for a French invasion was not only to be found in London.

After a grand parade, 10,000 Lancashire Volunteers had enjoyed the hospitality of Lord Derby and it was reported that they consumed 11,340 meat pies and 59 hogsheads of beer.

Anastasia knew that while such activities had delighted the cartoonists, there was a real fear amongst many of the Statesmen and Politicians who called on her mother.

Sir Charles Napier, who commanded the Baltic Fleet during the Crimean War, had declared in her presence,

"France is a greater danger than it has ever been since I was a boy, when the first Napoleon threatened the country with an enormous fleet and a million men at arms."

The Queen and the Prince Consort, returning from a Naval Review at Cherbourg in August of 1858, had told the Grand Duchess how perturbed they were by the immense warlike preparations of the French Navy.

When the first ironclad, *La Gloire* was launched in France late last year, the Queen had exclaimed in horror,

"Something must be done, and done quickly!"

"The diplomatic reports tell us that the Emperor Louis Napoleon is most acquisitive," Lord Palmerston had said to the Grand Duchess only last week when he had dined at Windsor Castle.

Anastasia wondered now if he had an ulterior motive in proclaiming to her mother his fear and anxiety about the French.

She did not need the Viscount, or anyone else, to tell her that the decision to marry King Maximilian to a relative of the English Queen was entirely a political manoeuvre.

Maurona was a small kingdom situated on the Gulf of Lions in the Mediterranean, with one frontier bordering on France, the other on Spain.

It had been an independent country for a great many years but, like Nice and Savoy, its larger and more important neighbours always overshadowed it.

"You understand why we must act quickly," Viscount Lyncombe said, breaking in on her thoughts. "You have to come away with me, Anastasia. If you say that you will do so, I will arrange everything. When will you go home?"

"Mama and I leave here tomorrow."

"Very well, I will take you away on Thursday."

"No – no, Christopher, do not talk like that!" Anastasia cried. "I cannot possibly decide anything so momentous while we are dancing, and besides, how can I be certain that what you are saying is true?"

"You will learn about it soon enough," the Viscount replied grimly. "You know as well as I do, Anastasia, that my father never speaks lightly without being sure of his facts."

That was true, Anastasia thought. As Lord-in-waiting to the Queen, and very much *persona grata* at Court, the Earl of Coombe never spoke in haste, and in consequence seldom said anything that was worth hearing.

If he had said that the Privy Council had decided to send her as a bride to King Maximilian of Maurona, she need not question that that was what would happen.

And yet it was hard to credit that her whole future had been decided so easily.

Although many people found Christmas at Windsor Castle a tedious and rather boring affair, Anastasia had always enjoyed it enormously.

In contrast with the very dull, very restricted life she spent with her mother in a 'Grace and Favour' house at Hampton Court Palace, the party at Windsor seemed both gay and exciting.

Certainly the bleak, cold, rather frightening Castle looked its best when decorated for the festivities.

The chandeliers were taken down in the Queen's private sitting room and big Christmas trees hung with candles and toffees took their place. The dining tables were piled high with food, and on the sideboard there was an enormous baron of beef.

In the Oak Room there was another Christmas tree, surrounded by presents for all the members of the household, and on each was a card written by the Queen herself.

This year the lake had frozen over and every day the party had gone to the ice to skate or to be pushed in an ice-sleigh, comfortably tucked in with a fur rug.

In the evening there were entertainments, a play performed by the Royal children, or an Opera given in the Waterloo Gallery where the acoustics were not very good. But to Anastasia, who very seldom was allowed to go to the theatre, it was a tremendous treat.

The performers and the orchestra had been brought down to Windsor by special train, but they were unfortunately taken back again immediately afterwards, leaving her no chance to talk to them and learn a little about their lives. Everyone's life, she had often thought to herself, was more exciting – and certainly less monotonous – than hers.

It was a joy to talk to new acquaintances whom she met at the Castle, and she laughed merrily at the Prince Consort who, when he was in a good humour, made puns and invented riddles.

Besides this, Anastasia found that, when he talked seriously on Naval matters and scientific subjects, she could always learn something that she wished to know.

Because the rest of the year had been so quiet and indeed so dull, she found everything at Windsor Castle amusing, even playing 'spillikins' with the younger children or the new 'round' game, *main jaune,* over which they would grow quite noisy, until the Queen called them to order.

What she had enjoyed more than anything else tonight was the reels or Scottish jigs, which she had danced with both spirit and grace, even though she was certain her mother would take her to task for it tomorrow.

"You must behave in a more circumspect manner," the Princess Beatrice would continually say to her daughter. But Anastasia could not help feeling that when she was old there would be time to behave in a circumspect manner, while for the moment she wished to enjoy herself.

"Well, have you made up your mind?" Viscount Lyncombe asked.

"You know quite well I have not," Anastasia replied. "I cannot just run off like that without giving it proper consideration."

"If I had any sense I would compel you to come with me," the Viscount said. "What was that fellow in the poem called who snatched up a girl, threw her across his saddle and galloped away with her?"

"You mean Young Lochinvar," Anastasia told him.

"He may have had an extremely stupid name, but he had the right idea."

"I am not being carried away on your saddle – which I am sure would be very uncomfortable," Anastasia said positively, "and without any gowns or any of the things I need to make myself look attractive."

"You look lovely whatever you wear," the Viscount said.

Now there was a deep note in his voice and a look in his eyes that made Anastasia feel a little shy.

At the same time it was fun to think she could so emotionally move the boy who had always teased her until at one period in her life he had made her hate him for it.

The ball was coming to an end, and as the couples that had been dancing stood facing each other, the Viscount said,

"What time are you leaving tomorrow?"

"Early in the morning, I think," Anastasia replied. "The Queen will have had enough of us by then."

"I will call on you tomorrow evening. I will bring a message from my mother, or it should not be too hard to think of some other excuse."

"Find out everything you can," Anastasia said. "I wonder if anyone has spoken to Mama about it?"

She was to learn almost as soon as they left the Castle the next morning that the Grand Duchess was, in fact, fully cognisant of what was being planned.

"I want to talk to you, Anastasia," she said, almost as soon as the Royal carriage that was to carry them to Hampton Court Palace had passed through the gates of the Castle and was proceeding down the hill towards the river.

"What about?" Anastasia asked, with a wide-eyed look of innocence.

"Your marriage."

"My marriage, Mama?"

"The Queen would have spoken to you about it herself," the Grand Duchess went on, "but she decided it would be best for me to talk to you first and explain how very fortunate you are."

Anastasia said nothing. She had learnt from long experience that it was a mistake to interrupt her mother once she had something she wished to express.

"As you have been well educated, Anastasia," the Grand Duchess continued, "there is no need for me to explain to you the political difficulties which face this country from French aggression and the terrible threat of invasion from those who we once thought were our friends."

"I do realise that, Mama," Anastasia said meekly.

"The balance of power in Europe is therefore of extreme importance and the French must not be allowed to acquire any more territory than they own at the moment."

"No, of course not, Mama."

"And that is why Maurona must be encouraged to remain independent by having a Queen whose sympathies are British."

The Grand Duchess spoke the last words very slowly to make them sound as impressive as possible, and after a moment's silence Anastasia asked quietly,

"How does that affect me, Mama?"

"You, Anastasia, have been chosen by the Queen to be the bride of King Maximilian!"

Before Anastasia could speak, the Grand Duchess said quickly,

"I know this will be a shock to you, and I know too, Anastasia, that you will be deeply distressed at the thought of having to leave me and England. But this represents all I have ever longed for where you are concerned. And I know that, were he alive, your dear Papa would rejoice, as I shall do, at the thought of your taking your place amongst the crowned heads of Europe."

"Why has the Queen chosen me, Mama?" Anastasia asked.

There was a moment's pause as if the Grand Duchess debated with herself whether she should tell the truth, and then with an unexpected smile she said frankly,

"You are much the prettiest Princess available!" Anastasia laughed.

"Having seen the others, Mama, I must protest that it is not saying much!"

The Grand Duchess looked away from her daughter's amused face to say a little severely,

"King Maximilian is known to be very fastidious. It was not possible to send him someone he would not have admired or who would not grace the throne of Maurona."

She was remembering, as she spoke, how the Queen had said,

"Anastasia is really too young and from all I have heard, far too frivolous for such an important position, but there is no one else. The Prince Consort and I have looked into the matter very thoroughly, and we can find no one who is both eligible for the position and who has the sort of attractiveness which, I am certain, Maximilian would consider essential in his wife."

"I am, of course, ma'am, very gratified by your choice," the Grand Duchess had said humbly.

She could not help feeling a little triumphant at the fact that the Queen had chosen Anastasia for such a responsible position.

Ever since the Grand Duke had been killed in an accident four years after their marriage, Princess Beatrice had made her home in England.

Hohlenstein had been annexed peacefully and without opposition by Prussia, and she had come back to her own country, bringing her only child aged two.

She had very little money, and as a Grand Duchess without a husband or a Duchy, she had no official position except in respect of her Royal blood and her relationship with the Queen.

She had been given a 'Grace and Favour' house in Hampton Court Palace, but she had always been made to feel she was the 'poor relation' and that she and Anastasia were dependent entirely on the benevolence and patronage of Queen Victoria.

The Queen had allotted a thousand rooms in the beautiful Tudor Palace as apartments for the widows or children of distinguished servants of the Crown, or Royal dependents.

Built by Cardinal Wolsey, the Palace had been given by him to Henry VIII, who married two of his wives there.

Princess Beatrice had truly loved her husband, and if she had mourned him excessively there had been little alternative and no inducements for her to do anything else.

The other occupants of the Grace and Favour houses were mostly very old, and it was only as Anastasia grew up that her mother realised what a restricted and monotonous existence they both endured.

Occasionally, perhaps once a year, they were invited to stay at Windsor Castle. The Grand Duchess received a few invitations to State occasions at Buckingham Palace. But as far as Anastasia was concerned, there were lessons with her Governesses and Tutors, and little else to occupy her time.

The Grand Duchess had a few friends remaining from her girlhood days who occasionally asked her to stay, although they usually found a woman without a husband was difficult to fit into their house parties.

The Coombes were an exception, and when her childhood friend invited the Grand Duchess, Anastasia went with her.

The Grand Duchess would not have been a woman if she had not sometimes wondered whether it would be possible for Anastasia to make a match with the wealthy and charming only son of the Earl and Countess of Coombe.

But she had known it was only an insubstantial dream because Anastasia, as a Royal Princess, could not marry without the consent of the Queen, and Her Majesty always said categorically that no Royal personage should ever marry a man not of Royal blood.

But now Anastasia was to be a Queen, and the Grand Duchess felt her heart overflowing with gratitude for the fate that had brought this unexpected bounty to them both when she had least expected it.

"I wonder what would happen if I refused?" Anastasia said in a clear voice as the carriage passed by Eton College.

Through the window she could see the beautiful Tudor redbrick buildings that had housed the sons of gentlemen for centuries.

"Refused?" her mother ejaculated. "What can you mean, Anastasia?"

"Do you not think it rather barbarous, Mama, in this day and age, when we are supposed to be democratic, when men fight and die for freedom, that a woman can be ordered to marry a man she has never seen or spoken to?"

"How can you say anything so ridiculous?" the Grand Duchess asked. "You know as well as I do that Royal marriages are always arranged, as are indeed those of the aristocracy in civilised countries."

"I do not call it very civilised," Anastasia sighed. "In fact if you ask me, Mama, I think it is rather like being sold across the counter of a shop."

She laughed as she went on,

"The Queen has in effect said to King Maximilian, 'you want protection and help from England? Well, in that case, we will send you one of our very special brides packed up neatly in the Union Jack'."

"Anastasia! You will give me a heart attack!" the Grand Duchess exclaimed in a faint voice. "If the Queen heard you speak like that, she would be furious – absolutely furious!"

"I am not likely to say it in front of her, Mama," Anastasia replied. "I am only telling you what I think."

"Then do not think it, Anastasia. Can you not realise what a wonderful opportunity this is for you?"

Anastasia did not reply, and the Grand Duchess gave a little sigh.

"I know, dearest, how dull it has been for you these past few months since you have grown up. I had hoped that after you had been presented in the spring the Queen might make a special effort to ask you to dinners and parties at Buckingham Palace. But she did nothing about it."

"I do not think Her Majesty approves of me, Mama," Anastasia said blithely. "They always say she does not like anyone too pretty about the place."

"Anastasia!" the Grand Duchess exclaimed again.

"It is true! You know perfectly well that ever since the scandal of Lady Flora Hastings, when they thought the poor woman was having a baby, but in fact she died of cancer, the Queen has been frightened of pretty Ladies-in-Waiting."

"How can you speak of that regrettable and unfortunate episode?" the Grand Duchess enquired in shocked tones. "Who told you about it?"

"As you and everyone else in Hampton Court Palace whispered about it for years, of course I heard about it," Anastasia replied. "And, as you know, Lady Flora's aunt lives only three doors away from us."

"She should not have related anything that happened before you were born," the Grand Duchess protested.

"Old people have long memories," Anastasia said shrewdly, "and they always like to talk about things which happened when they were young. I was only telling you, Mama, why the Queen does not like me."

"It does not matter whether the Queen likes you or not. Anastasia," the Grand Duchess snapped. "She has shown that she has your well-being at heart, and that is all that matters. What is more, Her Majesty has actually offered to help me with your trousseau."

Anastasia gave a little cry.

"I don't believe it! Oh, Mama, imagine being able to have some really pretty and expensive gowns for once. I am sick to death of the ones we have made ourselves, and poor old Mrs. Hawkins is really past being a seamstress. Her fingers are so crippled with arthritis that I feel a brute if I ask her to undo a seam or take in a tuck. It is obviously agony for her to use a needle."

"We have not been able to afford anyone better," the Grand Duchess said almost apologetically.

"I know that, Mama, and I am not complaining," Anastasia said quickly, "but it would be wonderful to go to London and choose something really exquisite. How much did the Queen say she would spend?"

"She did not restrict us to a price," the Grand Duchess replied. "She just said she would give you half a dozen evening-dresses, a dozen day *toilettes*, twelve of everything you require underneath, and your wedding-gown."

"Now *that* is exciting!" Anastasia cried. "More exciting than being told I have to marry a King who has a *penchant* for French women and very likely dislikes the English."

"Anastasia!" the Grand Duchess exclaimed again. "How can you make such a statement? Who has told you such things about King Maximilian?"

"Now, be truthful with me, Mama," Anastasia said. "Have you not heard that the King has a leaning toward the French, which is why the Queen is so agitated in case Maurona should become part of the French Empire?"

"I cannot think where you have heard – " the Grand Duchess began, and then, as she met her daughter's eyes, she added reluctantly. "I have heard that the King is often in Paris."

"French women are dark, Mama, dark, attractive and very gay! Do you think the King is likely to admire me?"

The Grand Duchess looked at her daughter and found it difficult to reply.

Although Anastasia had a Russian name because the Czar had been one of her Godfathers, and her father had come from Eastern Europe, there could have been no one who looked more English.

She had two very blue eyes, the pale blue of a thrush's egg, in a small, heart-shaped face. Her eyelashes were very long and dark, while her hair had the gold of spring sunshine and seemed, even on the dullest day, to have an unusual light about it.

Her bones were small and she was very graceful – something she herself believed had been inherited from one of her father's ancestors, who were Austrian.

But her mother was English and her father's mother had been English, so with her pale pink-and-white skin seeming at times as translucent as a pearl, Anastasia was the living embodiment of what most people quite erroneously believed, was a typical English beauty.

Perversely, perhaps merely to confound her critics, instead of conforming to the general belief that a pretty face means an empty brain, Anastasia was extremely intelligent.

She was also sensitive and, her mother thought with a little pang of fear, very vulnerable.

'How would Anastasia,' the Grand Duchess asked herself now for the first time, 'knowing nothing of the world, so young, so innocent and ignorant of the problems and difficulties of diplomacy, cope with a man like King Maximilian?'

Then sharply she told herself that she had been supremely happy in her own marriage, even though it had been arranged in somewhat similar circumstances.

Granted, the Grand Duke of Hohlenstein could hardly be compared in importance or authority with the King of Maurona, yet she left England to marry a man she had seen only once, and she had fallen in love with him soon after they were married.

At the same time her upbringing had been very different. She had been one of a large family, she had brothers and a father whom she had loved and with whom she had had a close companionship, and she had in fact been twenty-two before she married.

Choosing her words with care, the Grand Duchess said now,

"I think, Anastasia, that while a man might admire one type of woman, when he is seeking amusement, he will wish his wife to be different not only in appearance, but also in character."

"That is a consoling thought, Mama," Anastasia answered. "But Lady Walters tells me that men usually fall in love with the same type of women, just as some men like Labrador dogs while others prefer Dalmatians!"

"Lady Walters!" the Grand Duchess snorted. "I have told you before now, Anastasia, not to spend so much time talking to that woman. I have never understood how she managed to obtain accommodation in Hampton

Court Palace. I can only think that the Queen has never met her."

"Oh, but she has, Mama! Lady Walters has often told me how snooty Her Majesty was, trying to give her a 'set-down' and finding it difficult as Lady Walters is so much taller."

"I have no desire to discuss the woman," the Grand Duchess said, "and I do beg of you, Anastasia, not to talk to her about your forthcoming marriage."

Anastasia did not reply because she had every intention of finding out from Lady Walters a great deal more about King Maximilian.

The widow of a distinguished Diplomat, Lady Walters was a walking fund of gossip that concerned every country in the world and every personage of any importance.

She was very old now and yet she insisted on wearing a bright red wig and used cosmetics, which the Grand Duchess and the other inhabitants of the Grace and Favour houses denounced with horror.

Lady Walters was amusing. She could make Anastasia laugh over the scandals that had taken place in every Court at which her husband had been Ambassador.

If she was somewhat spiteful about the Queen of England, it was understandable, owing to the fact that on her husband's retirement both he and she had been ignored or snubbed in Court circles.

As the carriage drove on towards Hampton Court Palace, Anastasia thought eagerly of the many topics she would now want to discuss with Lady Walters.

Yet she could not help remembering how vehemently the Viscount had inveighed against the idea of her being married to the King.

'Christopher is jealous!' she told herself.

At the same time she knew he would not have taken up such an attitude merely because he loved her.

There was no doubt that he genuinely did not approve of the King, and she wondered exactly what indiscretions His Majesty had committed, and if the anxiety he had aroused in the Queen was entirely due to the position of his country on the map.

As they journeyed on she thought of what she had heard about Paris and the gaiety and the extravagance of the Second Empire.

It was then she recalled that two years ago the Emperor Napoleon III and the Empress Eugenie had come to England to stay at Osborne with the Queen.

The Grand Duchess had been invited to meet them, but of course, Anastasia herself had been too young. She had, however, taken a most tremendous interest in the visit and begged her mother to tell her every detail of what had occurred.

The Empress's gowns were fantastic and Anastasia had searched the illustrated magazines for sketches of them. The following year the Queen had visited Cherbourg but, unfortunately, the Grand Duchess had not been included in the party to cross the Channel.

But Lady Walters had learnt all the details from one of her cronies. She told Anastasia how there was no smile and – certainly not the usual kiss – from Her Majesty for the French Foreign Minister's wife, Madame Walenska.

"Why not?" Anastasia enquired.

"Her liaison with the Emperor has become too widely known to be overlooked," Lady Walters replied.

"You mean that the Emperor – "

"My dear, he is a Frenchman," Lady Walters intimated with a smile. "There is not a beautiful woman in Paris on whom the Emperor does not look with interest. And who would be likely to refuse a man in such a position?"

Anastasia had thought over what she bad been told and had known it was something she had never dreamt about in her quiet, uneventful life.

Her mother had always led her to believe that once people were married they lived happily ever after.

But here was the Emperor of the French – a man who had lived in England and until the new talk of the invasion had been extremely popular there, being unfaithful to his beautiful and glamorous wife.

It was not difficult to encourage Lady Walters to talk of the women who had charmed the Emperor of the French, and who made no secret about receiving his favours and the presents he showered upon them.

Sometimes Anastasia thought Lady Walters forgot that she was so young and knew so little of the world, and talked to her as if she was one of her contemporaries.

"Do you remember so-and-so?" she would ask, and then reel out a whole chapter of scandal, intrigue and passionate love, while Anastasia listened wide-eyed.

'King Maximilian is not a Frenchman,' she told herself now. 'But if he admires French women and the French way of life so wholeheartedly, I suppose it is natural for him to follow the Emperor's lead in affairs of the heart.'

For the first time she thought to herself there was some justification for the Viscount to have spoken as he had. Would she be wiser to run away with him, as he had suggested, rather than to risk finding herself isolated in a foreign country and married to a husband who was interested in some fascinating, dark-haired French woman?

Perhaps not one, but a dozen of them, if Lady Walters was to be believed about his *affaires de coeur*.

"Think how splendid it will be, Anastasia, for you to be a Queen!" the Grand Duchess was saying. "I believe Maurona is a beautiful country. The climate is delightful and, if you are married within a month or so, you will arrive in time to see the spring flowers, the oranges and lemons growing on the trees and the mimosa in bloom."

"Married in a month, Mama?" Anastasia questioned, sounding slightly startled.

"Perhaps I did not tell you," the Grand Duchess said evasively, "but the Queen is very insistent that no time should be wasted. After all, if the French Army decided to march into Maurona, there is nothing that the King could do to stop them!"

Anastasia knew then that the Viscount's secret information was correct.

It was not only the fate of Nice and Savoy that perturbed the Privy Council, but also the fate of Maurona. That was why she had to be married so speedily.

That was why England had to declare forcibly, in a way that the French would understand, that they were interested in Maurona remaining independent! And why not, when there was an English Queen on the throne?

'I am just a cat's paw,' Anastasia told herself. 'I am not a person. I have no individual importance. I am just part of a diplomatic game. If France takes a step forward, so does Britain.'

She thought again of how vehement some politicians were about the French intention of invading England.

The whole suggestion had seemed somehow unreal – an idea drummed up by the newspapers and alarmists like Lord Houghton, who had declared,

"The French eagles might stream from every steeple from Acton to Ealing and from Ealing to Harrow."

'I don't believe it!' Anastasia had thought at the time.

Despite the enthusiasm of the Volunteers and the noise they made drilling around Hampton Court Palace, she felt a French invasion was very unlikely!

Anyhow, it did not concern her.

And yet now her whole life was to change because of a French monarch's ambition and desire for conquests.

She was to be a Queen – a Queen like the one they had just left behind them in Windsor Castle.

There was no doubt that Queen Victoria adored her husband!

Anastasia had only to watch the way she looked at the Prince Consort and the manner in which she deferred to him to realise that she loved him very deeply.

But then, Anastasia thought to herself, the Queen had not only invited the Prince to come to England on a visit, before she allowed him to propose to her, but she had also had the choice of several other Princes.

'I have a choice,' Anastasia told herself now, 'to run away with Christopher, which would cause a terrible scandal, or to marry King Maximilian who does not want me and is interested not in the English but only in our enemies – the French!'

She drew a deep breath and then decided that what she had been about to say to her mother was best left unsaid. She knew quite well that the Grand Duchess's arguments would be based entirely on a desire for her own importance in the future. As far as feelings and emotions were concerned, her mother would expect her to be quite prepared to accept marriage as something that every woman desired, with or without love.

'Christopher loves me, but I do not love him,' Anastasia thought. 'The King may actively dislike me, except that we have not met, so how can I know what I feel about him until I see him? Then it will be too late.'

It seemed to her that she was in an extremely difficult position, and yet there was no one who could help her or even advise her what to do about it.

The Grand Duchess went on talking all the way to Hampton Court Palace, but Anastasia was not listening.

She was confronting the first big problem in her quiet life.

Then, as they saw the beautiful, centuries-old red brick Palace in front of them and passed through Anne Boleyn's gateway, she thought with a little lilt in her heart that whatever decision she came to, it would be exciting.

Her dull and uneventful existence had come to an end. Ahead was adventure, but she felt as if she stood at the top of a mountain and whichever way she jumped could prove disastrous!

'But anything,' Anastasia told herself, 'anything, and any man is better than staying here cooped up in these small rooms with interminable lessons and no one to talk to except old men and women waiting to die.'

"Here we are – home again!" the Grand Duchess exclaimed. "And now, Anastasia, we have a great deal to do. We must make an immediate list of your requirements and arrange to visit London tomorrow."

She gave a deep sigh, as if of relief.

"It is exciting, is it not, dearest?"

"Very exciting, Mama!" Anastasia said truthfully.

Then, as she walked in through the door of their apartment, she wondered with a little feeling of fear whether the Palace in Maurona, if she were married to a man who did not love her, might not prove even more of a prison than the Grace and Favour house at Hampton Court Palace had always seemed to be.

Chapter Two

As soon as Anastasia had helped her mother take their cloaks and personal bags upstairs while the coachman carried up their trunks, she slipped into the drawing room.

She wanted to search amongst some magazines, which she knew were lying on a shelf in the Chippendale book cabinet. She vaguely remembered seeing, some weeks ago in the *Illustrated London News,* a picture of King Maximilian and after glancing through half a dozen back numbers she found what she sought.

It was a full-page representation of the King showing him in uniform, wearing innumerable decorations and with a ribbon over his shoulder.

Anastasia stared at the portrait for some time, trying to make up her mind what she felt about it.

It was difficult to judge whether King Maximilian was as striking-looking as the artist obviously intended him to be. He had a square forehead above a straight, classical nose and what looked like a determined chin. His dark eyes looked straight ahead and Anastasia thought there was something stern about his expression.

He looked rather intimidating and very unlike any man she had ever seen. He was definitely foreign-looking and different from the English men she was accustomed to, though not in the least like a traditional Frenchman or Spaniard.

'Perhaps,' Anastasia thought, 'his features owe something to both his Greek and Roman origins.'

She had been remembering, while her mother chatted beside her in the carriage, that Maurona had a long history of invasion and conquests.

The Greeks, who were a sea-faring people, had early established a colony in Maurona. They were succeeded by the Phoenicians who, at the height of their power, conquered all along the coasts of the Mediterranean.

The Romans, Anastasia thought, must later have left many buildings behind them, and she vaguely remembered reading somewhere about the discovery of a great Roman Amphitheatre in Maurona.

But all this was in the past.

What she was considering now was the reigning King Maximilian III, who had inherited from his father a prosperous country – and one that was fiercely patriotic.

That was all Anastasia remembered, but when she looked at the caption beneath the King's portrait, she read –

"King Maximilian III of Maurona, who has been visiting Paris as the guest of the Emperor Napoleon III and the Empress Eugenie. His Majesty is a frequent visitor to the French Capital."

One always got back to the same point where the King was concerned, Anastasia thought, which was that he was very pro-French.

She shut the *Illustrated London News* up and put it back where she had found it. She did not wish to discuss the portrait of the King with her mother. She just wanted to learn more about him.

She realised it was still early in the afternoon and that Viscount Lyncombe would not be arriving until later.

Anastasia tiptoed across the drawing room and reaching the small hall with its narrow staircase, she listened. She could hear her mother talking to the old maid who looked after them, and she thought they would be unpacking.

So, very quietly, she opened the front door and slipped outside.

The red bricks of Hampton Court Palace were glowing like jewels in the winter sunshine. There was a feeling of frost in the air. Later, when the sun went down, it would be very cold, but for the moment Anastasia felt as if it renewed her vitality, so that even after her long drive from Windsor Castle she was not tired.

She ran as quickly as she could along the Broad Walk to the door, which led to Lady Walters's apartments.

She did not question whether Lady Walters would be pleased to see her, for she knew that the old woman was always eager for visitors and would be longing to hear about the Christmas party at Windsor Castle.

A servant so old that his livery hung on him as if it covered a skeleton rather than a body let Anastasia into the apartment.

But the crested buttons, which had once seen the inside of many different Embassies were polished brightly, and the ancient retainer had a toothless smile on his wrinkled face as he went ahead of Anastasia towards the Drawing room.

"Her Royal Highness, my Lady!" he announced in a stentorian voice that, owing to his deafness, was far too loud.

What appeared to be a bundle of shawls seated at the fireplace stirred and a quavering voice asked,

"Who? Who did you say?"

Then Lady Walters saw Anastasia.

"Oh, it is you, my dear!" she exclaimed. "You are back! I was remarking only this morning that you had said you would return today. I am so glad to see you."

Anastasia approached the armchair. Lady Walters was wrapped in several woollen shawls and her knees were covered by a very motheaten and patchy sable rug.

But the colour of her face showed that she was still cold and the blue-veined arthritic hand she held out to Anastasia was like ice.

"How are you, ma'am?" Anastasia enquired.

"Very old!" Lady Walters replied. "But let's talk about you. Did you enjoy yourself at the Castle, and did her plump little Majesty still look as usual like a pouter-pigeon?"

Anastasia laughed and, because she knew it was expected of her, related all they had done and what the Queen had said to her. She made it sound more amusing and gay than it had in fact actually been.

Lady Walters, her red wig a little askew, sat listening to every word.

She was not as deaf as might have been expected at her age, although Anastasia knew that she was not above pretending to be hard of hearing when she was bored.

Now, being determined to miss nothing of what she was being told, she heard every word that Anastasia spoke in her soft musical voice.

Anastasia's recitation of the Christmas Festivities came to an end, and she paused before she said in rather a different tone,

"I have something to tell you."

"What is it?" Lady Walters asked. "Are you going to inform me you have fallen in love with that dashing young Viscount? I have been expecting it!"

"No, I have not fallen in love with him," Anastasia answered.

"But he would like you to, no doubt," Lady Walters said with a little cackle of laughter.

Anastasia did not reply and the old woman went on,

"He will not be allowed to marry you. The Queen does not hold with love-marriages, except where she herself is concerned, and as she is known as the most inveterate matchmaker in Europe, she will doubtless, sooner or later, find a husband for you."

"She has already," Anastasia said in a low voice.

"She has?" Lady Walters cried. "Who? Who has she chosen? The Ruler of one of those German Principalities? Heaven knows, there are enough of them! The 'Thums and Thars' my husband used to call them, since he could never remember their names."

"No, it is not a German," Anastasia said.

"Then who? Who?" Lady Walters questioned.

"King Maximilian!"

"Of Maurona," Lady Walters cried. "I had forgotten him! Well, I think he should do nicely for you. You will like Maurona. It's a lovely country. My husband and I once spent a week there when we were travelling from Marseilles to Gibraltar."

She was silent for a moment as if she were looking back into the past and trying to remember what had happened.

"The present King's father was alive then, a fine-looking man, but very stiff. The parties at the Palace were deadly, no one could speak unless they were spoken to and we had to stand for hours."

"And you saw the present King?"

"A nice young man, handsome, with good manners. He seemed somewhat subdued and suppressed in those days – but from all I hear he has changed considerably in the last five years."

"Tell me about him," Anastasia asked.

"Do you want the truth, or what would please you to hear?"

"You know me well enough, ma'am, to know that I want the truth," Anastasia replied.

Lady Walters gave another cackle of laughter.

"That is what people always say until they hear it! At the same time, you will have a lot to cope with from all I have heard."

Anastasia drew in her breath.

"And you think I can 'cope' with it, as you say?"

"Why not?" Lady Walters asked. "You are pretty enough to make any man's heart beat faster! That always been an essential preliminary step in getting the elusive male into our clutches."

She saw the expression on Anastasia's face and went on,

"It is no use your looking like that, my girl! All women want to capture and enslave a man. You are no exception."

"Is it – possible where a marriage is – arranged?" Anastasia faltered.

"What else do you expect it to be where Kings and Queens are concerned?" Lady Walters asked. "Even a King is human, and you are very human, my child, unlike some of those stuck-up, snooty Royals who behave as if they were a race apart!"

She cackled again and said,

"As my husband always used to say – 'they bleed if you prick them and all of them have to blow their noses when they have a cold!'"

Anastasia laughed, she could not help it.

"I knew I should not be frightened if I talked to you about it," she said.

"Frightened? There is nothing to frighten you," Lady Walters said. "You will be a Queen and even these days that amounts to something. Whatever else, it ensures a great deal of material comfort."

"Tell me more about King Maximilian," Anastasia begged.

"Strangely enough," Lady Walters answered, "I was talking about him only a month or so ago to a friend of my husband's who had just arrived here from Paris."

"He was there at the same time as King Maximilian?" Anastasia asked.

"He was indeed. He was telling me about the women who are causing such a sensation in the *'Gay City'*. Vulgar lot of creatures they seem to me, but with the Emperor behaving like a small boy let loose in a sweetshop and what can other men do but follow his example?"

"Tell me about these – women."

"What do you think your mother would say?" Lady Walters enquired.

"There is no reason for Mama to know what we say to each other."

"I should hope not!" Lady Walters said, "and I doubt if the Grand Duchess even knows of the existence of *'les Grandes Cocottes'*."

She paused, glancing at Anastasia's intent face as she continued,

"There have been *courtesans*, my child, since the beginning of time. In fact, as one of the mediaeval Bishops said, *'Every City must have its sewer!'* But from all I hear the Parisian variety have achieved a place in Social history which is different from any they have occupied in the past."

"Why?" Anastasia asked.

Lady Walters considered for a moment.

"I think it is a question of a man's desire to show off," she replied slowly.

After a moment she went on,

"In England a man spends his money on horses, which are a symbol of his wealth, his taste and his expertise. In France a Frenchman chooses a mistress with the same discrimination."

"It seems – strange," Anastasia murmured.

"I think it is nothing short of lunacy," Lady Walters replied. "Great fortunes are poured out at the feet of these common women, most of who come from the gutter. They parade themselves in the *Bois* and at the *Opéra* with an ostentation that would be considered disgusting in any other great Capital."

"Then why not in Paris?"

"Because the Emperor himself encourages it," Lady Walters replied. "In fact they say he cannot resist a pretty woman and that every *courtesan's* ambition is to attract his attention."

"And do they love him when he does notice them?" Anastasia enquired innocently.

"Love!" Lady Walters ejaculated. "There is no such word where *cocottes* are concerned. The most famous of them, '*La Paiva*', if rumour is to be believed, loves only money, and hates men, children and animals unless they can provide it. Yet there is more money spent on her than on the defence of France!"

Anastasia looked incredulous and Lady Walters went on,

"She wears two million francs' worth of diamonds, pearls and precious stones. I am told that the house which is being built for her in the *Champs Elysée* by her present lover will cost a million and a half."

"Can that be true?" Anastasia exclaimed in amazement.

"Why not? My friend was saying that Cora Pearl, who came from the slums of Plymouth, is so extravagant that an Irishman spent his whole fortune of eighty thousand pounds on her in a week!"

"It seems incredible!" Anastasia exclaimed. "Do the men who spend such enormous sums really feel it is – worthwhile?"

Lady Walters laughed.

"They are envied by their friends, and presumably they feel that they get their money's worth one way or another."

Anastasia was silent, digesting what she had heard, and Lady Walters continued,

"Noblemen, of course, who offer such creatures their protection, have more glamour about them than ordinary men, but nevertheless they are expected to contribute ropes of pearls, diamonds, or in the case of a Royal personage like Prince Napoleon, a house in a fashionable quarter of Paris or a *château* in the country."

Anastasia drew in a deep breath.

"It is difficult to – understand."

"You are asking me this," Lady Walters said, "because you are wondering whether King Maximilian, when you are married to him, will find Paris with one of *'les Grandes Horizontales'* more amusing than his Palace in Maurona, with an English wife."

"It is obviously a – question that will be in my – mind," Anastasia admitted honestly.

"The answer is, of course, entirely up to you," Lady Walters said.

"What do you mean?" Anastasia enquired.

"A clever woman can always hold her husband at her side. Look at the Queen. Do you think that pompous German Princeling has a chance of escape?"

"That is different," Anastasia said. "Everyone says that Prince Albert was very much in love with Her Majesty when they married."

Lady Walters snorted.

"In love! Who would not be in love with marrying England, even if it involved embracing a fat little creature who had been dragged up by an overpowering and disagreeable mother?"

"I am sure they are very happy," Anastasia countered.

"Just as you can be happy, my child, if you go the right way about it."

"What is the right way?"

"Make sure that he falls in love with you," Lady Walters said. "Once a man is in love he is like wax in a woman's hands, and it should not be difficult with your looks."

Anastasia gave a little sigh.

She was thinking once again that the Parisian women who attracted King Maximilian would be witty, vivacious and dark in colouring. But somehow she felt too embarrassed to ask Lady Walters any more.

She had been so anxious to learn about King Maximilian, yet now as she listened she felt that the garrulous old woman made everything seem rather cheap.

There was something almost unpleasant in the way Lady Walters described the *courtesans*, and Anastasia did not wish to hear any more about women who were so alluring that fortunes were cast at their feet by every man who looked at them.

It was, however, one thing to start Lady Walters talking and quite another to stop her.

"My friend was telling me," she cackled now, "that at one dinner party given for those Birds of Paradise, the grapes and peaches were arranged not on leaves, as might have been expected, but on thousand-franc notes which disappeared into the low-cut *décolletages*."

It seemed to Anastasia as she came away from Lady Walters apartments that it would be impossible to forget diamonds and rubies flashing against white necks, mountains of francs being poured out in an endless supply on gowns, horses, carriages, and noisy parties which only ended long after the dawn had broken.

It was difficult to know if everything Lady Walters said was true, and yet Anastasia could not help thinking that it was all too fantastic to be anything but factual.

Then despairingly she asked how she could ever compete in a world where such women reigned, where wild extravagance was not an occasional experience, but something which continued day after day and year after year in the one city in Europe where any rich man would be welcomed.

Then she told herself that even Kings might have other interests, and perhaps King Maximilian, when he was not in Paris, was concerned with governing his country well.

'I must learn everything I can about Maurona,' Anastasia told herself.

As she hurried back home, she realised that she had already made up her mind that she must accept the position to which the Queen had assigned her.

However, there was still the Viscount to contend with.

Anastasia wanted to see him alone, so, when she heard his carriage draw up outside about half an hour after she had returned from Lady Walters, she opened the door herself. Her mother was still upstairs in her room. The unpacking had been done, but she was now compiling long lists of the clothes that would be required for the trousseau.

The Viscount had driven his own horses from London and, when he stepped down and handed the reins to his groom, he saw Anastasia waiting for him in the open doorway.

Before he could speak, she put her fingers to her lips, and then, as he checked the words he was about to say, she whispered,

"Come in quietly. Mama is upstairs and I do not wish her to know you are here."

They walked very softly across the hall and Anastasia shut the door of the drawing room behind them.

The Viscount moved across the room to stand in front of the fire burning in the grate.

He was extremely well dressed, and Anastasia thought as she looked at him that he was nice looking. He was not handsome, but he had an air of breeding about him that was unmistakable.

"I have been making plans, Anastasia," the Viscount began in a low voice as she walked towards him.

"I too have been thinking, Christopher," she replied. "You know as well as I do that it is impossible for us to run away."

"Why should you say that before hearing where we can go?" he asked.

"Because, for one thing, you must not leave England," Anastasia answered. "You are an only son, Christopher, and one day you will have to take your father's place, not only as regards his title, but also his position at Court."

"You are making that an excuse to refuse me," the Viscount said harshly.

"I have to – do what the Queen and Mama – want," Anastasia said.

"It is what you want, too!" the Viscount said accusingly. "Like all females you dream of being a Queen. You think a crown on your head will make you happy, but it will not, Anastasia, not without love – and if you fall in love with Maximilian, he will break your heart."

"How can you be sure of that?" Anastasia enquired.

"Because I know him and I know you. You are too sensitive, too innocent to cope with a man like that."

"After all," Anastasia said in a low voice, "he cannot marry the women he sees in – Paris."

"Who has been talking to you about them?" the Viscount asked.

"Lady Walters was explaining to me about the extravagance of – "

Anastasia's voice died away.

She was not quite certain by which term she should refer to the women in question.

"Lady Walters should know better than to talk of such things to you," Viscount Lyncombe said sharply.

"From all I have heard she was considered very fast herself when she was young."

"Oh, was she?" Anastasia asked with interest. "I always suspected that might explain why she knows so much about – the – *Demi-Monde*."

"Anyone who has been in Paris knows about them," the Viscount interrupted.

"Then it is true! " Anastasia said. "All the things she has told me about the jewels, the parties, how the Emperor and King Maximilian dance attendance upon such – women."

"If they do, you should know nothing about it," the Viscount said crossly. "Ladies should not speak of such women. The Grand Duchess would be furious if she knew that you had heard such tales, especially where the King is concerned."

"You said much the same thing!" Anastasia retorted.

"That is different," the Viscount said loftily. "I was trying to persuade you, as I still am, Anastasia, to realise how very much happier you would be with me to look after you. I love you, and I swear that you will never regret it if you will run away with me."

His eyes were on her face, and because she felt a little shy at the sudden throb of passion in his voice she looked away from him.

"I think the truth is, Christopher," she said in a low voice, "that if I loved you, as you say you love me, I would willingly come with you and risk the consequences, but – I do not – love you."

"Why not?" he asked sharply.

Anastasia made a helpless little gesture with her hand.

"Perhaps it is because we have known each other since we were children. I don't know. I like you very much, and I will always have a deep affection for you, but I know in my heart it is not love."

She tried to smile and went on,

"That is why, although I am very grateful, Christopher, for your offer and for wanting to save me from what you think will be an unhappy marriage, I can only say no."

"And that is something I will not allow you to say," the Viscount said fiercely. "You know nothing about love, Anastasia, and nothing about men. I will teach you to love me."

He put out his hands as he spoke and drew her into his arms.

For a moment Anastasia was surprised, and then, as she realised he was about to kiss her, she struggled against him.

"No, Christopher! No!"

"I love you, Anastasia! I want you!"

She turned her head away so that his lips only touched her cheek, and at that moment the door opened and the Grand Duchess came into the room.

Anastasia and the Viscount started guiltily and moved apart.

But the expression on the Grand Duchess's face as she moved towards them told Anastasia she had seen what was occurring.

"You did not inform me, Anastasia, that we had a visitor," she said and her voice was icy.

"I – I was just coming to tell you so, Mama," Anastasia replied quickly.

The Grand Duchess looked at the Viscount.

"I am afraid, Christopher," she said coldly, "you have called at an inopportune moment. Anastasia and I have just returned from Windsor and we have a great deal to do."

"So I understand, ma'am," the Viscount said, "but I was anxious to speak to Anastasia."

"I am afraid that is not possible," the Grand Duchess replied as if Anastasia was not in the room. "As you will doubtless be told by your father, Anastasia is to be married very shortly."

The Viscount's lips tightened, but he did not speak and the Grand Duchess continued,

"You will therefore understand, Christopher, that she will have no time to spare even for so old and valued a friend as yourself."

For one moment it seemed as if the Viscount would defy the Grand Duchess and then, as he met her eyes, he capitulated.

"I understand, ma'am."

"Then you had best say goodbye to each other," the Grand Duchess said. "I am sure Anastasia is very grateful for the kindness and hospitality your father and mother have shown her all through her childhood. I am certain, too, she will always welcome you to her new country, whenever you are in that part of the world."

There was something stern and inflexible about the way the Grand Duchess spoke, which made the Viscount as well as Anastasia realise that nothing either of them could say would be of any avail.

Anastasia realised that the Viscount was hurt and upset at being more or less thrown out of the house, but there was nothing he could say – and indeed nothing he could do except leave.

"As I am obviously in the way, ma'am," he said to the Grand Duchess, "I will return to London."

"You know as well as I do, Christopher, there is no alternative."

And Anastasia was aware that her mother had guessed what the Viscount had come to say.

She looked at him pleadingly, hoping he would understand that she was sorry this had happened, and that after so many years of friendship he was being treated in a somewhat cavalier fashion.

She put out her hand and to her surprise he lifted it to his lips.

"Goodbye, Anastasia," he said and his voice was unsteady.

Then he turned and went from the room.

The Grand Duchess did not move.

She and Anastasia stood silent until they heard the front door shut and a moment later there was the sound of wheels and the horses' hoofs.

"How could you, Mama?" Anastasia said in a low voice.

The Grand Duchess moved across the room with a rustle of her silk petticoats.

"I do not intend to discuss this with you, Anastasia," she said. "All I can say is that I am extremely surprised at your behaviour. I can only be thankful that I came downstairs when I did."

She went from the drawing room leaving Anastasia alone, and only after standing still for some minutes did Anastasia put her hands up to her face.

'Have I made the right decision?' she asked herself. 'Would I have been wiser to go with Christopher, however difficult the future might be?'

*

It was, however, impossible to worry about the Viscount for during the next weeks there was so much to do that every night Anastasia was exhausted when the time came for her to go to bed.

There were first of all innumerable trips to London to choose clothes, to fit them and to indulge in an orgy of shopping such as she had never experienced before.

Besides this there was an incessant stream of visitors, some of them so distinguished that Anastasia had never expected them to condescend to someone so unimportant as herself.

The Prime Minister requested the Grand Duchess to bring Anastasia to number 10 Downing Street, but Lord John Russell, the distinguished Foreign Secretary, called in person at Hampton Court Palace.

"I do not need to tell Your Royal Highness," he said, "the political importance of your marriage, because I am quite certain that your mother has explained that to you."

"Yes, she has told me that the independence of Maurona concerns the balance of power in Europe," Anastasia replied. "But I think, my Lord, you have other reasons for wishing this marriage to take place so quickly."

Lord John Russell's deep-set eyes searched Anastasia's lovely face.

"What secrets have you been told?" he asked with a faint smile.

"I heard that you were worried that the Emperor might annex Nice and Savoy."

"That is the truth," the Foreign Secretary replied, "but we would not wish it to become general knowledge."

"It will not, as far as I am concerned," Anastasia told him.

"Your Royal Highness is very young," Lord John went on, "but that is not a disadvantage. With your beauty and charm you can do a great deal to influence the King to pay more attention to the interests of his Spanish subjects rather than those of French origin."

Anastasia looked a little puzzled and he explained,

"You must realise from the position of Maurona on the map that the Pyrenees make a natural barrier which divides the country in two. Although the Mauronians are extremely proud of the fact that their history is steeped in antiquity, there is no doubt that continual infiltration across their frontiers has influenced the feelings and aspirations of the people."

"I can understand that," Anastasia said.

"As a result," Lord John continued, "you have a population at times deeply divided amongst themselves with the Crown as the only bond that unites them."

Anastasia did not speak and Lord John went on,

"I was in Maurona last year and I found quite an unusual amount of ill-feeling in the Spanish part of the country where the people think they are being neglected or overruled. They want consideration and, to put it bluntly, more personal interest from the King."

"I understand," Anastasia said quietly.

"If you can go out of your way to please the Spanish population of Maurona, then I think you will win the hearts of a people which, in my opinion, is among the finest in the world," Lord John finished.

Again Anastasia murmured that she understood and she had the feeling that when Lord John Russell left the house he was pleased with her.

The Prime Minister said little of significance when they called at number 10 Downing Street.

There were too many people there for them to have an intimate conversation and Anastasia had the feeling that he had only wished to see her and be assured in his own mind that she would do what was expected of her.

She found Lord Palmerston charming, very much a lady's man, and she could understand, after the flattering words he said to her, why he was nicknamed 'Cupid' amongst his friends.

There was so much to do, so much to think about, that Anastasia could hardly believe it when she realised that she had only two more days in England before she was due to embark on the British battleship, which was to carry her to Maurona.

Once again she realised it was a political move for her to be sent to her new country by battleship rather than to travel overland.

It was like taking part in a theatrical performance, she thought to herself. She was the heroine, but her part was stereotyped and there was no room for individual moves or personal interpretation of the part she had to play.

The greatest statesmen, the finest political brains in England, were composing her lines, and they had chosen all her appearance, her scenery and props.

She could not help feeling a little more afraid of the unknown future every day.

It was impossible not to be overawed by the responsibility that had been placed on her shoulders, and by the knowledge that the Prime Minister and his Cabinet were depending upon her to save Maurona from being swallowed up by the greed of the French Emperor.

'I cannot do it!' Anastasia longed to cry. 'I am too small and insignificant! It is all too big and overpowering, and when I fail, as it seems inevitable I must, you will blame me!'

She knew that such an outcry would only be attributed to girlish nervousness, if in fact they listened to her at all. She was just, as she had told herself at the beginning, a 'cat's-paw'.

All she had to do was walk on to the stage pronouncing the lines she had been taught and making the movements they expected of her.

In simple words, she must behave as a puppet rather than as a real person.

'I have ceased to have any identity of my own,' Anastasia told herself more than once when she went to bed.

Because she felt afraid, she took from where she had hidden them the letters Viscount Lyncombe wrote to her nearly every day.

She had bribed the old servant to bring them straight upstairs to her when the post arrived to ensure that her mother did not see them.

They were very passionate love letters, and she found it difficult to believe that they had really been written by the boy she had known all her life and who had teased her about her mosquito bites.

"1 love you, Anastasia! Christopher had written over and over again. I love you! Come away with me, I want to hold you in my arms and kiss you. I want to awaken a fire that I know is there inside you so that you will love me as much as I love you!

We will be happy anywhere in the world so long as we can be together. I will take you to the West Indies so that we can be in the sunshine. We will visit China and Japan. We can see Russia and travel back through Europe.

Everything would be amusing, wonderful and gay if you were with me! It is all I ask of the future, that we can be together, and I swear that if you will trust me and come with me, I will make you very happy."

There were over a dozen letters all saying very much the same thing, and, when she read them, Anastasia could not help feeling unhappy because she must hurt Christopher.

He had been so much a part of her life that over and over again she asked herself if in fact she did love him.

What would she have felt, she wondered, if he had kissed her as he had meant to before her mother came into the room?

Anastasia had never been kissed, but she had always imagined it would be something very wonderful and that a man's lips would awake in her a wonder such as she had read about in books and poems.

And yet when Christopher had tried to kiss her, she had instinctively struggled against him and she had known she did not wish him to do so.

Why? Why?

It was really the least she could have let him do when they were to be swept apart, perhaps never to meet again.

But something deep inside her told her that what she felt for Christopher now would never turn into love.

She could see he was attractive, she could see he was a young man for whom most girls would feel a fluttering of their senses, a rising excitement and a throbbing of their hearts.

Yet, although she liked him so much, when he touched her it meant nothing.

She had danced with him, she had held his hand, she had even for one moment been close in his arms, and nothing had happened.

"Perhaps I am naturally cold," Anastasia told herself.

Lady Walters had often laughed at cold women.

"She has as much feeling as a flatfish!" she had said of one woman whom she disliked, and of another, "She is like a piece of cold marble."

Because she was worried about *herself*, Anastasia attempted to talk to her mother.

"What did you feel, Mama, when you became engaged to Papa?"

"I was very happy, Anastasia."

"But you were not in love with him – the marriage was arranged and you did not even know if he was in love with you."

"Your father was *extremely* handsome," the Grand Duchess said. "I think that almost as soon as I saw him I fell in love, but I was very shy and it took time for us to get to know each other. Afterwards, as I have told you so often, we were extremely happy."

"And Papa excited you?" Anastasia asked.

The Grand Duchess was still for a moment and then she said,

"I do not know who has been talking to you, Anastasia, but a lady always conducts herself with *reserve* and control. Her husband would not expect otherwise and would undoubtedly be shocked!"

"Would that not be rather dull, Mama?"

"No, of course not!" the Grand Duchess said positively. "If one is well-bred, Anastasia, and especially if one is Royal, one must not be overemotional at any time. I have spoken to you about this before and you know as well as I do that to show lack of restraint in public would be a *betise* beyond description."

"I was not thinking of what one – would do in – public Mama."

"The same applies to when one is in private. A man wants to honour and respect his wife, and a King particularly would not expect the woman who sat beside him on the throne to behave like some common creature in the street!"

"Is it common to fall in love, Mama?" Anastasia enquired.

The Grand Duchess obviously chose her words with care before she responded,

"I think, Anastasia, you are quite intelligent enough to realise that romantic and passionate love as it is portrayed in novels does not happen to everyone. It is more often than not an illusion. But one can have friendship, pride and deep affection for the man with whom one shares one's life. It can be far more important than seeking sensations that have no substance in fact."

There was a long silence between mother and daughter, and then Anastasia said in a very low voice,

"Will you tell me, Mama, how a man and a – woman make – love together?"

The Grand Duchess stiffened.

"That, Anastasia is something your husband will explain to you," she replied coldly after a moment. "It is sufficient for you to know that after you are married anything that occurs between you and your husband has the blessing of God. Apart from that it should not be thought or talked about at any time."

She rose to her feet as she spoke and went from the room without another word.

Anastasia stared after her in bewilderment!

Once again she told herself despairingly that she might have been wiser to accept the Viscount's plea that they should run away together.

Chapter Three

"Good morning, Your Royal Highness!"

Anastasia opened her eyes to see Olivia, the maid who had been sent from Maurona to attend her, curtsying in the doorway of the cabin.

It would have been more dignified if she had not had to hold on to the door as she did so because the ship was pitching violently, as it had done ever since they turned from the English Channel into the Bay of Biscay.

In fact the storm had grown worse day after day until, even though being in a battleship gave Anastasia a sense of security, she wondered at times if they would not founder or 'turn turtle'.

The rest of the party had succumbed to seasickness completely.

When Lord John Russell and various other Statesmen of importance were seeing them off from Tilbury, Anastasia had done her best to appear dignified.

The Grand Duchess had been the very epitome of dignity as, warmly wrapped in furs, she descended from the Royal carriage that had conveyed them from Hampton Court.

She had greeted the party who were there to bid them farewell with graciousness and at the same time a slight touch of condescension, which told Anastasia without words exactly how her mother had behaved when she had been the reigning Grand Duchess of Hohlenstein.

She herself had been too excited at the thought of the journey ahead to worry for long about the impression she created.

But it was rather awe-inspiring to realise how distinguished and important the gentlemen were who had come to wish her 'God Speed' on what, apart from anything else, was the most important voyage of her life.

The battleship *H.M.S. Warrior* looked very impressive.

It was, Anastasia had been told, Britain's answer to *La Gloire* and was the largest vessel in the world. It had been built by private contract by the Thames Iron Works and Shipbuilding Company.

As she looked at the battleship she was to board, the First Lord of the Admiralty came to her side to say,

"This will be the *Warrior's* first voyage, and I hope she will prove as comfortable for your Royal Highness as has been predicted."

"She is armour-plated, I believe," Anastasia said, anxious for him to know that she was aware that the *Warrior* was an exceptional ship.

"She is indeed," the First Lord replied, "and the weight of her armour alone is one thousand, three hundred and fifty tons!"

He smiled as if he thought he was being too technical.

"It was during the Crimean War that the effectiveness both of armour-plating and of shell fire was demonstrated."

"I have read what terrible damage shellfire did to unarmoured wooden vessels," Anastasia said in a low voice.

"Unfortunately, the quickest to learn the lesson were the French," the First Lord said. "As I expect you know, *La Gloire*, the first sea-going ironclad, was launched last year."

"I am sorry we could not have been the first," Anastasia remarked.

"The *Warrior* is an improvement on her rival," the First Lord said quickly, "and we have two or three other vessels being constructed on the same lines."

"She looks very large."

"Her total weight is eight thousand, nine hundred tons," the First Lord explained, "nearly three times that of the wooden line of battle ships she has displaced."

"I am very honoured to be the first traveller on the *Warrior*."

Anastasia smiled as she spoke and she saw what she recognised as an unmistakable glint of admiration in the First Lord's eyes.

It was not surprising that the crowds who had gathered at the quayside cheered as Anastasia went aboard.

Dressed in rose pink, her jacket trimmed with fur and her bonnet decorated with pink ostrich feathers, she looked very romantic and very lovely.

"Good luck!"

"Here's to yer happiness!" the crowd shouted, and as she walked towards the gangplank small bunches of white heather and a silver cardboard horseshoe were thrown at her feet.

The party who were to escort her to Maurona, consisting of her mother and Sir Frederick Falkland, the British Ambassador to Maurona, had been augmented by the Baroness Benasque, who was to be her Lady-in-Waiting, and Captain Carlos Aznar, who was an *aide-de-camp* to the King.

Besides these personages who had travelled overland from Maurona to England, there was also Olivia, the maid who was to look after Anastasia on the voyage.

She said proudly that she had been chosen because she came from a sea-faring family, and was never unwell at sea. It proved to be a great blessing because the Grand Duchess and Sir Frederick were not to be seen almost from the moment the ship left harbour, and the Baroness, after struggling white-faced for two days against the uneasiness of her stomach, finally capitulated and retired to her cabin.

"Is the storm worse than ever?" Anastasia asked now as Olivia drew back the curtains over the porthole.

"It is still exceedingly rough, Your Royal Highness," Olivia replied, "and the Captain has sent a message suggesting that it might be wisest for you not to rise from your bed in case you should break a leg."

"I have every intention of getting up," Anastasia said positively. "I must go on with my lessons. I am determined by the time I reach your country to be able to speak fluently to my new subjects."

"Your Royal Highness is learning fast," Olivia answered. "You must have a natural aptitude for languages,"

Anastasia smiled with satisfaction.

It had pleased her to find that Mauronian was not as difficult as she had anticipated. It was in fact a mixture of French and Spanish, based on Latin, and as she was proficient in all three languages, Mauronian seemed to come quite easily to her tongue.

At the same time she had applied herself to learning the language with an enthusiasm and a strength of will which was indefatigable.

She talked to Olivia and, more important, she made Captain Carlos Aznar, the only one of the Mauronian party on his feet, give her lessons which lasted nearly the whole of each day.

"I shall tire you, ma'am," he had protested more than once.

"I don't mind being tired," Anastasia replied. "I am determined to be proficient by the time we reach Maurona."

"I cannot tell you how gratifying it is, ma'am, to hear someone speak in such a way," he said and there was a note not only of appreciation in his voice but undoubtedly of another emotion as well.

After five days at sea, Anastasia was well aware that the Captain was falling in love with her.

There was that unmistakable expression in his eyes and a note in his voice she had perceived in the Viscount, and it gave her a feeling of comfort to realise that to at least one Mauronian she appeared attractive and desirable.

It would have been unthinkable in ordinary circumstances for her to spend so many hours alone with an attractive young man who had merely been sent as an escort with his other duties undefined.

It should have been the Baroness who sat with Anastasia and instructed her, and the Baroness who should have told her all she wanted to know about her new country and what awaited her on her arrival.

As it was, Captain Aznar was only too delighted to answer any questions Anastasia put to him.

"Tell me about your Capital," she suggested.

"Sergei is on the French side of the Pyrenees," he answered, "but only just, with the mountains towering up above it. It is also our largest port."

"The Palace is attractive?" Anastasia enquired.

"It was originally a castle, and part of what remains of the old Palace is hundreds of years old," he replied. "But about fifty years ago His Majesty's grandfather built an entirely new Palace on the old site. It is extremely impressive and modelled on the Palace at Versailles."

"Again a French influence!" Anastasia remarked without thinking.

She saw the expression on Captain Aznar's face darken as he replied,

"There is another Palace at Huesca on the other side of the mountains, which is like the Alhambra in Madrid."

"Does His Majesty often go there?" Anastasia asked.

"It has not been used for many years," Captain Aznar replied.

This, Anastasia was sure, was the bone of contention.

She had already learnt that Captain Aznar's family was of Spanish origin and he was passionately devoted to the part of the country south of the Pyrenees.

'It must have been deliberate,' she thought to herself, 'that while the Baroness is of French persuasion, Captain Aznar is Spanish.'

Whoever had chosen her attendants had tried to be impartial.

She had learnt from Olivia that while she came from Sergei and had worked in the Palace for some years, she also was a Spanish-Mauronian, as her dark skin and black hair suggested.

As the girl helped Anastasia to dress she talked of the beauty of her country, but it was quite obvious she was speaking about the Southern Provinces and the olive groves like those over the Spanish border.

"I want you to help me, Olivia," Anastasia said now, as the maid arranged her hair, occasionally finding it difficult to keep her balance as she stood behind Anastasia's chair.

Fortunately, everything in the cabin had been battened down, but even to put a brush on the dressing table was to have it flung violently to the floor, while the waves beat wildly and tempestuously against the portholes as if they were trying to break the thick glass.

"You know I'll do anything Your Royal Highness asks of me," Olivia replied in her warm voice.

"When we are in Sergei, I want you to tell me what the people think about me."

She saw the surprise in the maid's eyes and went on,

"It is very difficult to learn the truth, when one is surrounded by courtiers who say what they think you want to hear, and by those who wish only to be pleasant. I am going to rely on you, Olivia, to tell me what I should know. It is the only way I can help your people."

"It's Your Royal Highness's wish to help us?" Olivia asked in a low voice.

"I want it with all my heart," Anastasia replied with a note of sincerity in her voice that was unmistakable.

She saw Olivia draw in her breath.

"Your Royal Highness is a very wonderful lady. I'm very grateful for the privilege of serving you."

Anastasia did not say anything more at the moment but she was determined to impress upon Olivia that she must not be afraid to speak openly, not only all through the voyage, but once they arrived at the Palace.

'I shall be a stranger in a strange land,' Anastasia told herself, 'and I must have help.'

She had seen enough Palaces to realise that the occupants lived behind plate glass windows.

They had little personal or real contact with those they ruled because those who served and protected them against anything harsh or unpleasant wrapped them in cotton wool.

'If I don't learn of what is likely to occur before it happens,' Anastasia thought, 'then there will be no chance of my doing anything to prevent the French from marching in.'

It was all very vague in her mind and she had no idea what she could do, but she was determined, if it was possible, not to return to England an exile and a failure.

She knew how deeply her mother had suffered since she had been a widow without a country, compelled to live on the charity of her relatives.

'That must not happen to me,' Anastasia told herself.

With a little quiver of fear she remembered that if ever she did have to leave Maurona, then the King would be with her.

It was horrifying to think of returning to England defeated and unwanted, but even worse to imagine what it would be like with a frustrated and resentful husband.

So often, when there was news from Hohlenstcin, the Grand Duchess would say to Anastasia,

"I thank God that your father did not live to see this day!" or "how your Papa would have hated to know that all he had worked for has been forgotten or changed!"

'I will fight to save Maurona,' Anastasia told herself every night before she went to sleep.

Then, even as she said it, she thought how insignificant and ineffectual she was, just one ignorant girl who knew little about life and who had seen nothing of the world outside England.

'Why did I not learn more?' she asked herself a dozen times, and it was little consolation to realise that she was in fact far better educated than most girls of her age.

Now, as she applied herself to learning Mauronian, she thought it was only the first step in what she already thought of in her heart as a crusade.

"Tell me more! Tell me everything you think I ought to know," she said to Captain Aznar when she found him waiting for her in the Admiral's cabin.

It was far more comfortable than Anastasia had expected, and, as they settled themselves in two velvet covered armchairs that were battened to the floor and faced each other across a table that was fixed in the same way, she saw the irrepressible admiration in Captain Aznar's eyes.

"I thought that after such a rough night, ma'am," he said, "you would not brave the elements this morning."

"Was it worse last night than the night before?" Anastasia enquired.

"One of the Officers has just told me that he thinks the storm has blown itself out, but it was exceedingly unpleasant after midnight."

Anastasia looked embarrassed.

"I am almost ashamed to say I was sound asleep!"

"You are amazing, ma'am! I never thought a woman could show such fortitude."

"I am so delighted to find that I am a good sailor."

"You have never been to sea before, ma'am?"

"Never," Anastasia answered. "But as I had no wish to miss my lesson, I was determined to keep on my feet!"

"That has been almost an impossibility," Captain Aznar said with a twinkle in his eyes, "but let us get to work."

He opened the book that he had in front of him, which Anastasia knew had been brought aboard by the Baroness. After they had gone through some of the verbs, it seemed simpler and much more pleasant to converse in Mauronian.

"I never believed anyone could learn as quickly as you have done, ma'am," Captain Aznar said after they had been talking for nearly an hour.

"I think it is a very pretty language," Anastasia answered, "and I want you to tell me more about what must be a very pretty country."

After Captain Aznar had talked for some time, Anastasia said a little hesitatingly,

"C-can I – trust you, Captain?"

The Captain's eyes opened in surprise before he responded,

"I should be very distressed, ma'am, if you did not believe that you could do so."

"Of course I do believe it," Anastasia answered, "but I want you to tell me quite frankly, forgetting for the moment the position I shall hold, what I can do to help Maurona."

The Captain was silent for a moment and then he said,

"You speak, ma'am, as if you had already heard that we have difficulties."

"I have learnt that there is unrest amongst those who live South of the mountains," Anastasia replied. "They feel they are not on equal terms with those who – shall we say – are more influenced by their French neighbours."

At first Captain Aznar seemed to choose his words with care, but then he began to talk rapidly with an eloquence and a sensitivity that told Anastasia how deeply he felt in the matter.

He told her how the more important positions in the Government Departments were always given to those with French sympathies, how there was more constructive development in the North of the country than in the South, how trading concessions always appeared to be granted to those of French lineage.

"What is more," Captain Aznar continued, "the nobility and upper classes habitually speak French, so that our own language is gradually going out of use and being forgotten."

Anastasia could realise this was an important point.

"The Prime Minister is passionately committed to Maurona," Captain Aznar went on. "But many of his colleagues favour the view that the country might fare better if more closely affiliated with France."

He paused to add forcibly,

"To me and to a number like me that would prove utterly and completely disastrous."

"What is the position in the Army?" Anastasia asked.

"There, things are much more equal," Captain Aznar conceded. "But then, the Army is usually stationed in the South. The great plain of Leziga lies just below the Southern slopes of the mountains where manoeuvres always take place, and new barracks have been built there, so that the Army, one might say, is more acclimatised to the Spanish Region."

"They are loyal to His Majesty?"

There was a significant pause before Captain Aznar replied,

"I believe so. I am telling you the truth, ma'am, when I say I really believe so, although there has been a little unrest from time to time when His Majesty has been abroad."

There was no need for the Captain to explain that the King was spending too much time out of his country – and there was certainly no need to tell Anastasia where he went.

"Lord John Russell spoke to me of your difficulties," she said, "and you know only too well how very hard it will be for me to alter the status quo. I would be much criticised for trying to do so. I have told myself that I am a foreigner and as a foreigner I must move very very carefully in case I do something unacceptable."

"I cannot express to you, ma'am, what it means to me to hear you speak like this," Captain Aznar said. "When first I saw you, I thought – "

He stopped.

"What did you think?" Anastasia prompted.

Again Captain Aznar hesitated before he said,

"I thought you were the most beautiful woman I had ever seen! But I also thought, and please do not think I am being rude, ma'am, that you were far too young and too inexperienced to think of anything but pretty gowns, balls and parties."

"But now?" Anastasia asked.

"Now I think you will capture the hearts of everyone in Maurona," he said in a low voice, and there was no need for him to add that his own heart was already completely captivated.

*

The bad weather continued until they reached the Straits of Gibraltar.

It was then that Anastasia learnt that the battleship had suffered some superficial damage during the storms, which must be repaired before they could finish the last part of their journey.

She was not perturbed.

She was enjoying herself on the *Warrior*, and as far as she was concerned there was no hurry to reach Sergei.

Baroness Benasque struggled up on deck looking white-faced and a physical wreck after being so seasick, and exclaimed in horror at the delay.

"This will mean," she said, "that unless they postpone the date of your marriage, ma'am, which I think is impossible, you will have very little time in Sergei before the wedding."

"Does that matter so much?" Anastasia asked lightly.

She thought to herself that however long the interval between her first meeting King Maximilian and the day he became her husband, it would make no difference to the final issue.

Even if they disliked each other on sight, there was nothing either of them could do about it.

She had been sent off from England with great pomp and circumstance and she had been told of the preparations that were being made for her arrival and subsequent marriage.

Anastasia had already made up her mind that she must not anticipate too vividly what lay ahead, or dwell on potential difficulties so that she became afraid.

'I have to be calm, sensible and intelligent about all this,' she told herself.

But she could not help a little cold shiver of fear deep down inside her. It was hard to imagine what she would feel when she met her future husband, so she kept thinking of his face in the portrait.

In the meantime she was ready to enjoy Gibraltar!

The moment the English Garrison stationed there learnt that *H.M.S. Warrior* would be docked for two or three days while the storm damage was repaired, the Commanding Officer called with a request that Anastasia would attend a ball to be given in her honour.

After her inactivity at sea, she was longing for exercise and could imagine nothing more exciting than the opportunity of dancing with a number of charming young men.

The ship's Officers, who had had an exhausting voyage during the storm and no time to make themselves pleasant to Anastasia, were only too delighted to accept the invitation, and the Commanding Officer hurried away to make the arrangements for the ball.

It was fortunate that, when he came aboard, the Grand Duchess was still too weak to leave her cabin.

When she did so, she told Anastasia that she had no right to accept an invitation to be guest of honour at a ball in Gibraltar when it was not on the programme arranged for them by the Foreign Secretary before they left England.

"How could it have been, Mama?" Anastasia argued, "when Lord John Russell had no idea it was going to be so rough in the Bay of Biscay?"

"I think it would have been more becoming, Anastasia, for you to have gone ashore to see the Rock and perhaps the famous apes, and then return to the ship."

"I think, Mama," Anastasia said gently, "it would have been very priggish, and what the sailors would call 'snooty' to have refused such a delightful invitation, and actually I think the decision was one for me to make."

The Grand Duchess looked absolutely astonished.

"Really, Anastasia, you must have become swollen-headed to speak in such a manner," she said coldly. "You are not yet a Queen."

"I shall be in a very short time, Mama," Anastasia said, "and it was as a future Queen that I was asked if I would permit the English Officers to give a ball in my honour."

Her mother was silent, mostly because she felt too ill to argue.

When the evening came, she refused to attend the ball, saying that she did not feel well enough.

Baroness Benasque was therefore deputed to go as Anastasia's chaperone, and Captain Aznar, of course, escorted them.

It was perhaps a good thing that the Grand Duchess was not present.

After a slight stiffness and formality during the dinner party given for Anastasia by the Commanding

Officer, she quickly managed to put everyone at their ease.

She chatted away, her eyes bright with excitement, a patch of colour on her cheeks, looking so entrancingly pretty that after the first conventional dance with her host, hopeful partners besieged her.

She wore one of her new gowns of green tulle. The multiple frills were ornamented with bunches of lilies-of-the-valley, and it was more becoming than any dress she had ever owned before.

There was no doubt that Queen Victoria would have been scandalised at the verve and energy which went into the Mazurkas, and it seemed to Anastasia that even the waltzes were played faster than they had been at Windsor Castle.

It was all very gay, she told herself, and very good for her morale!

"Why did you have to be a Princess?" one Army Officer murmured in Anastasia's ear as she swept round the room on his arm.

"I ought not to say this, ma'am," he went on, "and you will very likely have me shot at dawn, but you are the prettiest girl I have ever seen, and now when I compare every other woman I meet to you, I swear I shall never get married!"

Anastasia knew it was not only her charms which had loosened the young man's tongue so indiscreetly, but also the fact that he had imbibed a great deal of the champagne that was provided at the ball.

At the same time it was delightful for her to listen to compliments she had never had the chance of hearing before. At Windsor Castle or when she had been staying with the Earl and Countess of Coombe she had only met men who had always been far too conscious of her rank, or perhaps her surroundings, to speak of anything but commonplaces.

"I hope King Maximilian will realise how lucky he is," a Naval Commander said during the last dance of the evening.

"I am hoping the same thing," Anastasia said lightly.

"His Majesty would be blind, deaf and dumb not to appreciate what we have brought him from England," the Officer said with a note in his voice, which told Anastasia that he was quite prepared to be truculent about his convictions.

"Nobody has told me yet whether or not the English are popular in Maurona," she answered.

"Whatever they have been in the past," the Commander replied, "I can assure you, ma'am, Maurona is getting now what by rights should have been kept in England! If I had my way I would lock you up with the Crown Jewels! You are far too beautiful to be exported abroad!"

Again Anastasia was quite certain that the Commander would not have spoken to her in such a familiar manner aboard the *Warrior*. But Gibraltar seemed to be a 'no-man's land' where she was far away from England and had not yet reached Maurona.

Besides, when one was being whirled round the room to the music of a Regimental band it was very hard to remember to be strictly conventional.

When they were back on board Anastasia went to her mother's cabin.

"You missed a wonderful party, Mama!" she said enthusiastically.

"You look somewhat dishevelled, Anastasia," the Grand Duchess said coldly. "I hope you have not been dancing in a manner of which I would not approve."

"I hope not, Mama," Anastasia said evasively.

She kissed her mother goodnight and then she said, as if in answer to an unspoken criticism,

"I might as well enjoy myself, Mama. In a few days' time I shall be a staid married woman and you yourself wished I could have gone to more parties and balls in the London Season."

"That was different, Anastasia," the Grand Duchess replied. "You know quite well that your partners this evening were hardly of the nobility or your equal in rank."

Anastasia laughed.

"I am sure Papa would have said that all of them have to blow their noses if they have a cold!"

She smiled at her mother and whisked out of the cabin before the Grand Duchess could think of a reply.

Then, as she was about to enter her own cabin next door, she remembered she had left a book she was reading in Mauronian in the Captain's cabin where she had her lessons with Captain Aznar.

She opened the door to find the Captain helping himself to a drink from a 'grog' tray, which stood on a side table.

He stood to attention, clicked his heels and bowed.

"May I offer you a drink, ma'am?"

"I would like a little lemonade, if there is any," Anastasia said.

He poured her some into a tumbler and handed it to her.

"You enjoyed tonight, ma'am?" he asked with his eyes on her face.

"It was delightful!" Anastasia answered. "More fun than any party I have ever been to."

She smiled and added,

"Not that I have been to many."

"I cannot understand that, ma'am. Everyone in England must have longed for you to light their parties like a star."

"The people Mama would call 'everyone in England' did not concern themselves with a Princess of no importance living in a Grace and Favour house in Hampton Court Palace!"

Captain Aznar smiled.

"So now, Cinderella, ma'am, is not only going to the ball, but is also to marry Prince Charming!"

Anastasia walked across the cabin to look out of the porthole at the lights on the quay.

"You think that is what His Majesty will be?" she asked in a low voice.

"I hope so," Captain Aznar replied. "I want your happiness, ma'am, as I have never wanted anything before in the whole of my life!"

Anastasia did not reply and after a moment he added,

"And to help you find it, ma'am, I pledge myself to your service, now and for all time!"

There was a depth of emotion in his voice that Anastasia found very moving.

Slowly she turned round to look at him and the expression in his eyes made her drop hers.

"One day I may have to hold you to that promise," she said quietly.

"And when that happens I will be a very proud and grateful man," he answered. "I am ready not only to die for you, ma'am, but also to live for you!"

Again Anastasia's eyes met his and for a moment it was impossible to think of an answer.

Then she held out her hand.

"Thank you," she said very softly, "I feel that where I am going I shall need a friend."

Captain Aznar took her hand in his and spontaneously went down on one knee and kissed it.

She felt his lips against her bare skin and then, as he rose to his feet, she took her hand away and said in a very young and breathless little voice,

"Thank you! Thank you very much!"

*

It was late the next afternoon when the ship was ready to leave Gibraltar. The band played on the quay and there were crowds of people to wave goodbye.

Anastasia, wearing one of her pretty gowns, stood beside the Captain and waved in reply.

The cold, the rain and the storms had been left behind. Now there was continual sunshine, and as they moved along the coast the Mediterranean was as blue as the Madonna's robe.

"We are late! We are terribly late!" the Grand Duchess moaned, and her cry was echoed by the Baroness. Anastasia left them commiserating with each other over the disruption of the timetable and went up on deck.

For the first time she was enjoying a warm breeze in her face, and the ship was moving smoothly over the water. Smoke was belching from the *Warrior's* funnels, but the sails were also being set in place, the three masts silhouetted against the blue of the sky.

"It is lovelier than I thought," Anastasia said to Captain Aznar who had come to her side as she leaned against the ship's rail.

"It is indeed very lovely!" he answered, but his eyes were on her face.

"Does our being so late really matter?" she enquired. "Mama and the Baroness are making such a to-do about it."

"It will merely mean that you will be married the day after we arrive instead of waiting a week, as had been intended," he replied. "It would be impossible to cancel all the arrangements or postpone them."

"Why?" Anastasia asked.

"Because of the Royalty who have been invited from neighbouring countries and the people who will have travelled for days so that they can be in the Capital to watch the marriage procession."

He smiled as he continued,

"I imagine all work in Maurona will practically come to a standstill. They will not have had so much pageantry and excitement since the Coronation."

"What Royalty has been invited?" Anastasia asked.

"I am not certain," Captain Aznar replied. "His Majesty was still discussing the guest list with the Prime Minister when I left."

"You don't think the Emperor and Empress of France will be invited?" Anastasia asked.

"If they are, I should think it unlikely they will accept," Captain Aznar replied.

This was somehow reassuring. Anastasia did not know why, but she did not wish to meet Napoleon III.

She was sure that he was very much to blame for the difficulties that Maurona was having and, moreover, his behaviour towards England made her feel suddenly antagonistic towards everything French.

"I am sure the rumours that the French will invade your country are untrue," Captain Aznar said, as if he guessed what she was thinking.

"I hope so," Anastasia said. "Did you see the iron fortress in the Channel? There was something about it, with its holes for the guns, which frightened me. One could almost imagine it being our only defence against an invading Army."

"1 am sure that whoever is predicting that there will be an invasion of England is scaremongering!" Captain Aznar remarked. "The Emperor himself has said that he has no intention of doing such a thing."

"The question is, can one believe him?" Anastasia asked.

Captain Aznar did not answer and she knew that he had no real wish to defend the Emperor of the French or any Frenchman. It was just that he was trying to reassure her.

"Don't let us talk about wars, or the threats of war," she pleaded. "We have only a short time left. Tell me more stories about Maurona. That is what I like to hear."

"Folk tales?" he asked, "or real life drama?"

"Folk tales," Anastasia said firmly. "I have a feeling there will be plenty of drama to cope with later on!"

*

As if her words were prophetic, a day later, as the *Warrior* moved into the Bay of Sergei, a small fishing vessel rammed another and, amid shrieks and cries of distress, the two boats began to sink.

Apart from this incident, *H.M.S. Warrior* came smoothly into port, but because she was so big it was impossible for her to tie up alongside the quay and she had to anchor in the centre of the Bay.

Standing on deck, Anastasia saw for the first time the country that was to be her home.

She had expected it to be beautiful, but not as lovely as this.

The houses in the City were white against a background of dark green pines, jutting cypresses and silver grey olives. Towering above the town there were the mountains of the Pyrenees, not very high immediately near the coastline, but far in the distance there were high peaks dazzling white with the winter snow.

The Bay of Sergei was very beautiful with a beach of golden sand at the water's edge, but, as the *Warrior* came into sight, great crowds of people surged down towards the sea, lining the jetty and the promenades and even grouping themselves on the roofs of the houses and hotels that faced the Bay.

There was the clang of Church bells, the sound of sirens and ships' hooters ringing out as the battleship dropped anchor.

There were flags and brightly coloured bunting everywhere and Captain Aznar had already warned Anastasia to expect a profusion of flowers.

"It will not only be the week of your wedding, ma'am," he said. "It is also Carnival."

"What happens at Carnival?" Anastasia asked curiously.

"It is the Festival of Flowers. There are processions through the streets and a Battle of Flowers."

"How exciting! Shall I see it?" Anastasia asked.

"I expect, ma'am, you will watch the procession from the balcony at the Chancellery which overlooks the Main Street."

"And the battle?"

Captain Aznar laughed.

"You will not, ma'am, be allowed to take part in that!"

"How disappointing! Where do the flowers come from?" Anastasia enquired.

"Our country grows an enormous amount of carnations and all sorts of spring flowers."

"For sale?" Anastasia asked.

"They are of course sold in the market," Captain Aznar answered, "but the greater part of them is made into perfume."

"Perfume! I had no idea!" Anastasia exclaimed.

"The carnation, rose and violet scent you will be given in Maurona is the foundation for many of the perfumes that are sold all over the world as exclusive to the French."

"How interesting!" Anastasia exclaimed.

"I am told by those who know that our tuberoses are the best in the whole of the Mediterranean, and the women of Paris crave for tuberoses."

The Captain did not add, because he did not think it suitable for Anastasia's ears, that tuberoses were the flowers of sensual love and that the *courtesans* of Paris prized their fragrance more than any other.

"I must see the perfume being made," Anastasia enthused.

"It is very interesting," Captain Aznar replied. "They say that one thousand five hundred flowers go to make a single drop of the famous 'attar' and the perfume oils have been acclaimed, like those of Grasse, since the time of the Renaissance."

He saw that Anastasia was really interested and went on,

"You can watch the distillation, ma'am, in Sergei and also at Arcala, which is on the Southern side of the mountains."

"I will go there too," Anastasia promised and he looked at her gratefully.

Almost as soon as the *Warrior* had docked, a very smart white launch with the Mauronian flag fluttering in the stern came speeding out towards the ship.

Nervously Anastasia turned to the Captain.

"Will His Majesty be coming aboard?" she asked.

He shook his head.

"It is arranged that the King will meet you, ma'am, on the steps of the Palace. You will drive through the City in procession escorted by the Prime Minister and members of the cabinet."

He saw that the launch was nearing the *Warrior* and added,

"I think, ma'am, you should go below and be with the Grand Duchess and the Baroness when they arrive."

"Yes, of course," Anastasia agreed.

She went to the Admiral's cabin to find her mother waiting for her.

"Where have you been, Anastasia?" she asked sharply.

"I went on deck to see the ship come into harbour, Mama."

"Then you should have told me where you were going," the Grand Duchess said. "Do remember Anastasia, to behave circumspectly. It is very important for you to make a good impression. First impressions are always the most important."

"I will do my best, Mama," Anastasia said meekly.

It was reassuring to know that her pale blue gown was very becoming and her bonnet, trimmed with pink rosebuds like her small sunshade would, she was certain, not be rivalled by anything that could be bought in Paris.

At the same time it was impossible not to feel nervous as the first dignitaries of Maurona were piped aboard and escorted by the ship's Captain to the Admiral's cabin.

The Prime Minister was a distinguished looking man, growing bald, and with shrewd and, Anastasia thought, somewhat calculating eyes.

He greeted her in French, but, when she answered him in Mauronian, he was obviously delighted.

"Your Royal Highness can speak our language?" he enquired with surprise.

"I have a very able teacher," Anastasia replied, "and I hope I shall not disgrace myself by being ungrammatical."

"I am sure Your Royal Highness could never do that," the Prime Minister replied.

There was a long exchange of greetings, before the English party finally went ashore in the white launch to where the open carriages of the procession were waiting for them.

To Anastasia's delight not only were the horses decorated with flowers but also the carriages themselves.

She sat back against a hood covered with carnations and found that she was to travel with the Prime Minister sitting beside her, and Sir Frederick Falkland, resplendent with his ambassadorial hat trimmed with white cock feathers, and Captain Aznar opposite her.

Sir Frederick had made her a long apology when they reached Gibraltar for succumbing to seasickness.

She found him rather dull and uninteresting and wondered why, since Maurona was so important, a more inspiring Ambassador could not have been found to represent England.

At the moment Anastasia wanted to make a good impression on the Prime Minister.

However, it was difficult to talk above the noise of the cheering crowds once the procession had set out towards the Palace. It stood high above the town, encircled by green forestry, which made it look like a glittering jewel in a velvet setting.

The streets were transformed with banners, flags, arches of flowers and garlands of every shape and size.

On balconies filled with waving people there were patches of brilliant colour from shawls, bunting and streamers of coloured paper reaching to the streets below.

Carnations, roses, lilies and wild orchids were thrown into the carriage until they covered the floor and the rug over Anastasia's knees.

It was all very gay and the populace smiled, waved and cheered while Anastasia responded with a sense of rising excitement and delight.

"They look so gay and happy," she said to the Prime Minister.

"We are, on the whole, a very cheerful people," he replied, "and if I may say so, ma'am, you look exactly as we all hoped you would."

"How is that?" Anastasia enquired curiously.

"Like a Princess in a Fairy story," he answered.

He smiled and added,

"You must forgive me, ma'am, but our usual impression of the English is of very tall, supercilious ladies and gentlemen with protruding teeth, wearing, when they are abroad, the Scottish tartan!"

Anastasia's laugh rang out spontaneously.

"I know exactly what you mean," she said, "and some English people do look like that. I hope I am different."

"You are indeed very different, ma'am," the Prime Minister said and, as she turned to smile at him, she was almost certain that once again she had made a conquest.

They drove on through streets that seemed endless and because they were so full of people they all looked very much alike.

At last the horses began to climb, until Anastasia saw just ahead of them a huge white Palace.

It was very impressive and, as they turned in through the enormous wrought-iron gates decorated with gold, she saw a classical fountain, its water being thrown up iridescent in the sunshine, and beyond it a long flight of steps leading up to the main doors.

There was a red carpet and a resplendent guard of honour, and arrayed on the steps was an impressive gathering of elegantly dressed people.

The gentlemen, mostly in uniform, were covered with decorations, and the ladies wore enormous crinolines and held small lace-trimmed sunshades to ward off the bright rays of the sun.

Anastasia's carriage rounded the circle where the fountain played and came to a standstill at the foot of the steps.

As she stepped out she raised her eyes to see a tall figure in a white uniform come through the door of the Palace and start to walk down towards her.

She felt her heart give a thump and she realised she was frightened in a way she had never been frightened before.

The King was approaching, the stern, dark-eyed man of the portrait!

King Maximilian III of Maurona – her future husband!

Chapter Four

"Kiss me again, *mon cheri,*" a voice said softly in French.

The man lying back with his hands behind his head on the silk cushions of the divan did not move.

"You are insatiable, Yvette," he said with a hint of laughter in his voice.

"If I am insatiable, you are irresistible!" came the reply. "It's getting late. You must go back."

"As a matter of fact it is early and I am in no hurry to face *today*."

She said 'today' with particular emphasis, and King Maximilian made a sound that was something like a groan.

"Is it really today?" he asked. "I had half hoped it would never come."

"Yes, it is today," the woman said relentlessly, "the day when my husband returns from Marseilles and your German bride arrives."

For a moment there was silence, and then the King said almost as if he was speaking to himself,

"I had not thought of her as being German, but English."

"Either nationality is distasteful," the woman said. "To the French the Germans are an unceasing threat, while the English – *helas!* How shall I describe the English?"

"I see no reason why you should describe them at all, Yvette," the King remarked.

"I detest the whole race!" Yvette le Granmont said passionately. "They are supercilious, arrogant and, I am delighted to say, their women are extremely unattractive!"

"I am told that my future bride is very pretty," King Maximilian remarked again, as if he was speaking to himself.

"And who could have told you?" the Comtesse enquired, and answered her own question. "Diplomats? Statesmen? Or doubtless the insufferable, autocratic Queen of England herself?"

She gave a light laugh, but there was no humour in it.

"I know how much such descriptions are worth because I am married to a diplomat, and what Henri says and what he thinks are two very different things."

"Let's hope that your husband neither thinks nor speaks where you and I are concerned, Yvette."

"I am very discreet," the Comtesse said in a soft, caressing tone, "and I cannot give you up, you know that."

"What do you expect my bride to say?"

The Comtesse laughed.

"She is young, presumably innocent, and to the pure all things are pure! Unless someone gossips about us to her, which I imagine is extremely unlikely, she will remain in blissful ignorance."

"We must behave with propriety, Yvette."

"And what do you mean by that?" the Comtesse asked. "Are you so afraid of the British lion in the shape of Queen Victoria, or should I say 'lioness'? What is it about that woman which enables her to have a finger in every pie in Europe?"

The King did not answer and after a moment the Comtesse continued,

"If you had any strength of will you would have refused this marriage, which has been thrust upon you against your every inclination. You know as well as I do that you have no wish to marry, *mon brave.*"

"That is indisputably true," the King agreed, "but as you say, I had not the strength of will to refuse the considerable pressure the British employed in making me marry the Princess they have chosen for me."

"*Mon Dieu*, it is too wicked, too unfair!" Yvette le Granmont cried. "But she can provide you with an heir while I will keep you happy and amused."

"I have a strange feeling," the King said, "that in English parlance that is not 'cricket'."

"The English! Always the English!" Yvette said petulantly. "Bah! They make me sick! If you had to marry, it should have been a Frenchwoman!"

"Unfortunately, there is no French Princess available," the King replied, "and besides, Queen Victoria would not have approved!"

Deliberately he spoke provocatively and with an exclamation of anger Yvette sat up.

She was wearing very little apart from the emerald necklace that echoed the green lights in her dark eyes.

Now, without bothering to turn his head, the King could see the curve of her breasts and the grace of her long neck, her piquant fascinating face, surmounted by a wealth of black silky hair.

He looked at her for a long moment and then slowly and without haste he swung his legs to the ground and rose from the divan upon which they had both been lying.

Covered with a number of silk cushions it was very Eastern in appearance and His Majesty had in fact copied it from one he had seen in the Palace of the Sultan of Morocco.

The rest of the room was typically French with its inlaid marble topped commodes, its gilt console tables and elegant carved mirrors.

There was a Boucher picture over the mantelpiece, a riot of blue, pink and soft toned flesh, and a picture by Fragonard on one of the other walls.

The room was in fact quite small. It was the King's private sitting room where no one was received without a special invitation.

Situated at a corner of the Palace at the end of his official suite it had the added convenience of a small staircase leading down to the ground floor, where there was a door that led out into the garden.

The King crossed the room and pulled back the draped satin curtains to look out.

"It will soon be dawn," he said. "You must go, Yvette."

"It is quite safe," she answered soothingly. "My carriage will be waiting for me the other side of the Palace wall and my servants are entirely trustworthy, I am sure of that."

"What you mean," the King said laconically, "is that they have assisted you in the past in such amorous escapades, and as they neither attempted to blackmail you nor informed your husband then, you suppose they are not likely to do so now."

"Why should they?" Yvette asked.

"Because for the moment I am in a particularly vulnerable position, as you well know," the King answered.

"You are worrying too much about yourself," the Comtesse replied. "Think of the Emperor. There is not a beautiful woman in Paris who has not entertained him in her own bed. I at least, come to you."

"For which, of course, I am very grateful!" the King said mockingly.

"Let me say again," Yvette said softly, "I have no intention of giving you up, *mon cheri*. Never has any woman had a more fantastic, more irresistible lover!"

Her voice was very caressing and the King turned from the window to look at her where she still sat on the divan, with only a diaphanous wisp of emerald green gauze to prevent her from being entirely naked.

He stood looking at her, and her eyes were on his face.

"What are you thinking?" she asked after a moment.

"I was wondering what it is about you that is so exciting," he replied. "You are an inveterate flirt, an unfaithful wife and, if I am not mistaken, your head will always ultimately rule your heart. What is it that makes you so alluring?"

"I can answer that question quite easily," the Comtesse replied. "It is because I burn with an unquenchable fire. What I can give you is something that your German-English wife will never be able to give."

"How can you be sure of that?" the King asked in an amused voice, his eyes still on her vivacious face.

"German women are stuffy, stolid and without a particle of imagination," she replied, "while the English are cold and very self-conscious, both of their bodies and of propriety. How can you imagine that passion can flourish on such barren ground?"

The King laughed.

"You are very voluble on the subject, Yvette. In a few hours we shall be able to ascertain if you are correct in your assumption, or whether Queen Victoria has been slightly cleverer than either of us anticipated."

"Cleverer? What do you mean by cleverer?" the Comtesse enquired. "Are you suggesting that your bride will be anything different from what I have described? *Mon Dieu! I* know the English, and their women have no feelings, none at all. Look at the Englishmen who come to Paris. What are they seeking? The amusement, the gaiety and the pleasures of the body which they cannot find in their own country."

"Perhaps you are right," the King said good-humouredly, "and undoubtedly Paris, as we well know, caters very extensively for what you call *'the pleasures of the body'*."

"But where you are concerned there is no need to go to Paris," Yvette said softly.

As she spoke, she held out her arms, but the King made no move to accept her invitation.

"It is too late for you to be here, Yvette," he said. "Go home. You must not be too fatigued to be pleasant to your husband when he arrives."

"I am always pleasant to Henri," the Comtesse said crossly, dropping her arms as she spoke. "Only the English cause scandals because when they are in love they have not the common sense to be pleasant to their marriage partners."

"I agree with you, it is a mistake," the King said, "and that is why I am telling you once again, Yvette, that you must return to the Embassy."

With a sigh the Comtesse le Granmont rose from the divan, then, as she stood draping her diaphanous green gauze around her, she gave a little cry and ran across the room to the King.

She reached up her arms and put them round his neck to draw his head down to hers.

"Je t'adore!" she sighed passionately.

Just for a moment her lips were against his, then he released himself from her clinging arms. She pouted at him and proceeded to pick up the rest of her clothes that were scattered on the floor.

When finally she was dressed in a negligee, which did little to conceal the nakedness of her figure, the King lifted from a chair a long cloak of black sables and placed it over her shoulders.

It covered her completely from her neck to her feet, and she pulled a green scarf over her loosened hair and tucked it under the fur.

"When shall I see you again?" she asked, and there was no doubt about the anxiety in her question.

The King shrugged his shoulders.

Then he answered her almost drily,

"Doubtless when with the rest of the Diplomatic Corps you receive the Princess tomorrow morning and at the Procession of Flowers in the afternoon."

"You know I do not mean that sort of occasion."

"When it is possible for you to come here," the King answered, "I will send you a message in the usual manner."

"You know I will be waiting to hear from you," she murmured softly.

She paused and then added,

"I am naturally consumed with jealousy! How I wish that I could be your bride instead of this milk-faced foreigner with whom you will have nothing in common."

"You are also a foreigner, my dear Yvette."

"But think how much we have in common," she countered quickly.

He laughed.

With his arm around her shoulders, he drew the Comtesse across the sitting room and opened the door in one corner. It revealed a staircase down which they could descend only in single file. At the bottom of the stairs was a very small square hall and a door opening on to the garden.

As they reached it, Yvette put out her arms and once again drew the King's head down towards hers.

"Bonne nuit, Roi de mon coeur!" she whispered. "Dream only of me. If nothing else, I claim priority in your dreams!"

"Goodnight, Yvette, and thank you for an enchanting evening."

He kissed her and then raised her hand to his lips.

He opened the door and she stepped out into the garden. Already the stars had faded and there was the first faint diffusion of light to herald the dawn.

It was easy to see the narrow flagged path leading down the avenue of cypress trees to where, at the end, there was a door in the Palace wall.

In the distance beside the door the King could see the cloaked figure of a man.

"Will you be all right?" he asked.

"My servants are waiting for me," the Comtesse replied. She walked away, her feet in her satin slippers making little sound on the flagstones.

After he had watched her for a few seconds, the King closed the door and went up the staircase to his sitting room.

The dented cushions looked somehow untidy and suggestive, and there was also the fragrance of Yvette's heavy, almost Oriental perfume on the air.

The King stood still for a moment as if he was thinking. Then he pulled open the door on the opposite side of the room and walked briskly towards his bedroom.

He imagined he would fall asleep as soon as his valet, who had waited up, had helped him undress, and he was lying in the huge canopied bed surmounted with a gilt crown in which the Kings of Maurona had slept for over two hundred years.

But sleep eluded him and he found himself thinking of Yvette and what she had said about his future bride. He wondered if she had been prophetic.

All the anger that he had felt since the moment he had learnt the Queen of England wished him to marry one of her relatives came surging over him like a flood tide that could not be controlled.

He had always intended to marry sooner or later, and was well aware that it was expected of him to breed sons to carry on the Monarchy.

But he had not expected to be dictated to or find himself in a position where it was almost impossible to refuse the directives of a foreign power.

But his country needed England's assistance both commercially and politically, and the price England had extorted for her favours was that one of Queen Victoria's descendants should sit on the throne of Maurona.

'I refuse! I categorically refuse!' the King had wanted to storm when he had been told what he had to do.

But long years of controlling himself under his father's rule had taught him to speak calmly and without heat, and to listen without comment to the arguments that were presented to him.

His brain, which had always been very astute, told him that there was no escape.

At the same time he disliked and resented the whole project to such an extent that it was hard to listen to the elation with which the alliance had been received and to accept the congratulations that had poured in from every side.

No one would attend when he had said over and over again in Council that there was no danger from the French. Had not the Emperor promised him personally that he had no interest in making any other conquests in Europe or annexing any territories?

"France is already large enough in all conscience," he had said when the King was staying with him in Paris. "It is difficult enough to rule peacefully that which I now possess and to ensure that economically we are a prosperous nation with a chance of becoming richer. What would I want with England or Maurona?"

"You are suspected of having designs on both!" the King had said with the frankness of a friend.

"I have been accused of so many sins I have not committed," the Emperor smiled, "so I suppose one or two more will not hurt me. But let us not talk politics, my dear Maximilian. While you are in Paris I have so many more beguiling subjects in which to interest you."

"So you do not want my throne?" the King had countered jokingly.

"God forbid!" the Emperor exclaimed in mock horror. "My own is precarious enough!"

They had both laughed and the King was now completely reassured that the fears of his Cabinet were as ridiculous and insubstantial as those that had caused the English to recruit a Volunteer Force and build iron fortresses in the Channel ready to repel a French invasion.

He thought of the amusements he had found in Paris and a smile curved his lips, as he lay sleepless against his pillows. Never had he imagined such luxury, such extravagance, and such beguiling and enthralling femininity as he had found in the 'Gay City'.

When he remembered how until the age of twenty-two, he had been compelled to stay in Maurona, a prisoner in the dullest and most pompous Court in Europe, he could hardly bear to think of those wasted years.

It was true that his father had allowed him to go abroad for the purposes of education, but always he had been accompanied by Tutors, Political Advisers, *aides-de-camp* and servants all chosen by his father and who, he was quite convinced, were also his father's spies.

He had never for a moment been allowed to enjoy himself freely. He had never been permitted to attend anything but the most formal parties that were arranged for him by his Political Adviser.

He met only those people of whom his father approved and the guest lists were brought back on his return for his father's perusal.

It was incredible to look back now and see how restricted and how monotonous his life had been.

Always he was supervised and controlled as he had been from the moment he left the nursery.

He was not even allowed to entertain boys of his own age without his father being present.

There were parties at the Palace to which sons of the nobility were invited to sit around while his father made conversation, or at special Festivals to watch Shakespearean or Greek plays chosen carefully by his father because they were of educational value.

It was not surprising that, as soon as Maximilian came to the throne, he wanted to see the world – and a different world from the one he had so far been permitted to view.

Three months after he was proclaimed King of Maurona he was in Paris and as the years went by his visits to the French Capital became more and more frequent.

He had stayed with the Czar of Russia and enjoyed himself in St. Petersburg and he had been a guest of the King of Greece and of the Sultan of Morocco.

He had found the protocol in the Palace of Schonbrunn in Vienna almost as stiff and as boring as in the Palace in Sergei during his father's long reign. So he had never returned to Austria, although he had been invited.

He had refused to visit England because he thought it would be a repetition of what he had endured in Vienna. He had been in England once when he was young, but he had found Prince Albert dull and formal and had hardly met Queen Victoria, as she had at the time been about to give birth to one of her numerous children.

England, he told himself now, was very much as Yvette had described it and that meant that his wife would bore him to distraction.

There was a scowl on his face as he thought of Anastasia. She was arriving late due to a storm in the Bay of Biscay.

'What a pity the ship could not have gone to the bottom! Then at least there would be a year's mourning before they could attempt to thrust another bride upon me,' he said to himself.

Trust an English battleship to come through safely!

The scowl grew even deeper.

He knew that those of his subjects with Spanish sympathies would think of the battleship bringing his bride to Sergei as a weapon of intimidation and warning to the French.

To the King it was an insult to his French friends, while to his Prime Minister it would be a confirmation of his conviction that it was wiser for Maurona to be linked with England rather than with France.

'Why are you so afraid?' the King had wanted to ask jeeringly at yesterday's Privy Council. 'What have you to fear except your own timidity?'

He had not spoken the words that trembled on his lips, but he had thought that the Prime Minister and those who supported him were like children scared of a 'bogey-man' which was nothing more substantial than a shadow on the wall.

The Emperor Napoleon III had given him his word. He had no designs on Maurona!

What else were they asking for and why should England be involved, and more intimately, himself?

The sun was flooding over the Bay and shimmering on the sea when the King finally fell asleep, and it seemed to him that he had only just closed his eyes when his valet called him.

"A lovely day, Your Majesty!" he called cheerily after he had drawn back the curtains, "and the crowds have been assembling all night."

"What for?" the King asked drowsily.

"Why, to welcome the Princess, Your Majesty! The Officer on duty has just informed me that the battleship has been sighted and should anchor in the Bay just before eleven o'clock."

The King did not reply, but after a few moments he flung back the bedclothes and got up in ill humour.

He was in what his nanny would have called one of his '*black moods*' as he ate his breakfast, hardly tasting the food that went into his mouth. He glanced with a jaundiced eye at the newspapers, which carried large portraits of himself, and a sketch of the Princess surmounted by a heart and garlanded with flowers.

The King looked at the picture without interest. It would not have been a very clear sketch in the first place and was badly printed, making her hair and eyes seem dark and the face somewhat heavy.

It was difficult to tell if the description of her as being pretty was, as Yvette had suspected, a diplomatic evasion, or the truth.

'Anyway,' the King thought to himself, 'it is immaterial. We shall have little to say to each other and certainly few interests in common.'

It was with bad grace that, after he had dealt with his correspondence with his secretary, he put on the resplendent uniform he knew would be expected of him.

"If you add many more decorations to the present collection," he snapped at his valet, "I shall look like a Christmas tree!"

"You must wear the Order of the Mauronian Martyrs, Your Majesty," the valet protested.

The King's mind caught on the word.

'That is what I am,' he told his reflection in the mirror, 'a martyr!'

Then he thought that whatever else happened as regards his marriage, he had no intention of being manipulated by his bride or dictated to, as her relative the Queen of England had done in forcing her upon him.

'If she is bossy and autocratic, she has a surprise coming to her,' he thought angrily. 'I will be master in my own Palace, even if I have some difficulty being master in my own country!'

Because he was feeling angry and aggressive he did not walk down the steps of the Palace until the very last second. He knew that his *aides-de-camp* were worried by the fact that, far from showing the eagerness expected of a bridegroom, he was deliberately delaying his appearance even in the hall of the Palace until the carriages arrived.

"The procession is turning in at the gates, Sire," one of his *aides-de-camp* said and there was no mistaking the agitation in his voice.

It would be an insult, as they all knew, if the Princess should descend from the carriage and start to climb the steps of the Palace before the King was even in sight.

When all those around him were looking at him imploringly and the carriage door had actually opened to allow Anastasia to step out onto the red carpet, the King passed through the Palace door.

With a slowness born of angry reluctance within himself, which he could not control, he started to walk down the red-carpeted steps between the ranks of the Guard of Honour.

Below him he could see a patch of pale blue and a figure that was definitely smaller than he had expected.

Down he went, step after step, and now the patch of blue was moving upwards towards him.

Anastasia was turning her head from side to side to acknowledge the greetings of the distinguished guests.

The women were sweeping low in their crinolines in a graceful billowing movement like the waves of the sea, while the gentlemen bowed their heads.

The same thing was happening on either side of the King as he descended, but he looked straight ahead. Now with almost perfect, if accidental, timing, King Maximilian and Anastasia met on the steps exactly half way.

She was conscious of the glitter of his decorations and then she lifted her face to look up at him. He was much taller than she had expected and as their eyes met for the first time Anastasia gave a little gasp.

Quite involuntarily she exclaimed,

"Oh, you look so much nicer than I had expected!"

For a moment the King was too astonished to reply.

Then, with a smile that swept away the scowl between his eyes, he said,

"May I be permitted, Your Royal Highness, to welcome you to Maurona? I am deeply honoured that you should come to my country and I can only pray that God will bless our union and that you will be happy here."

He took her hand as he spoke and raised it perfunctorily to his lips, but his eyes were still on her face. He had never imagined that anything, other than a piece of Dresden china, could be so pink, white and gold.

Anastasia's eyes were the blue of the wild forget-me-nots that grew on the alpine platèaux and her lips were smiling as, instead of replying to his formal speech of greeting, she, stammered in embarrassment,

"Forgive me for what I – said just – now, and please do not – tell Mama."

"She would not approve?" the King asked in amusement.

"She would be very angry. I had a formal speech prepared which I had learnt very carefully – but the awful thing is – I have – forgotten it!"

"I will not give you away," the King said good-humouredly.

"Please don't," Anastasia pleaded, "you have no idea how shocked they would be."

"Indeed I have a very good idea!"

Then they could say no more.

The private exchange between the Royal couple that had seemed deliberately contrived was now at an end, and the Grand Duchess took her place immediately behind Anastasia, the British Ambassador at her side.

"May I present to Your Majesty the Grand Duchess of Hohlenstein?" Sir Frederick said formally.

The King bowed over the Grand Duchess's hand as she rose from a curtsy and he then offered his arm to Anastasia. As she put her fingers lightly upon it, he led her up the steps and into the hall of the Palace.

"What are we going to do now?" she asked in a voice that only the King could hear.

"I present you to the Cabinet, the Members of the Household, the Diplomatic Corps and other influential people of Maurona," he answered.

"I hope I don't say the wrong thing," Anastasia whispered.

"You have only to smile at them," he assured her.

They moved through the hall and down a passage, which led into a huge salon that Anastasia realised, was the Throne Room, designed as a copy of the Hall of Mirrors at Versailles.

She had seen pictures of the French Palace and the imitation was unmistakable.

"I hear you had a very rough journey," the King said conventionally as they moved down the centre of the hall, seeing themselves reflected and re-reflected in the mirrors on either side.

"It was very disturbing for Mama," Anastasia answered. "Everyone succumbed except myself and Captain Aznar."

"I hope you found him entertaining."

"He was very kind and very instructive," Anastasia replied. "He taught me to speak Mauronian."

"I shall look forward to hearing you," the King answered in his own language.

"I only hope Your Majesty will not be disappointed or too critical."

"But that is good! Very good!" he exclaimed. "How could you have learnt my language so quickly?"

"I did not find it difficult. I am very anxious to understand your people."

The King looked at her with a faint air of surprise and she asked in a low voice that only he could hear,

"Am I what you expected?"

"Not in the least."

"The picture I saw of you was a very bad one. You looked stern and aloof and very inhuman."

"I can only hope that you will find me none of those things."

Anastasia smiled at him and he noticed that she had a dimple in her left cheek.

"I was very frightened when I saw you at the top of the steps," she confessed.

"And now?" he questioned.

"There are only half a dozen butterflies instead of six hundred fluttering inside me!"

He laughed and Anastasia glanced around apprehensively, quite certain that her mother would be frowning.

With an effort she forced herself to walk a little taller and then they reached the two gold thrones at the end of the hall.

They did not sit but stood in front of them on the dais, and the Grand Duchess with the Prime Minister and several *aides-de-camp* stood behind them. Looking back Anastasia could see that they had formed the head of a procession, which had followed them all the way from the Palace steps.

A resplendent official took up a position on her right and, as the notables one by one reached her, he announced their names and titles in stentorian tones.

First came the Cabinet headed by the Prime Minister, whom Anastasia had already met. Nevertheless she curtsied to him again, and as he raised her hand to his lips he said,

"I welcome you, ma'am, with even more sincerity than I did a little while earlier."

Anastasia smiled at him.

"You are sure I have not been a disappointment to the people?"

"You heard them cheering you," he answered, "and now they believe in Fairy Princesses."

The Foreign Secretary took his place.

"I had a letter from Lord John Russell this morning, ma'am," he told Anastasia. "He informed me how beautiful you are, but words are a poor substitute for the reality!"

"Do all Mauronians make such charming compliments?" Anastasia asked.

"When they have someone so very charming to say them to," the Foreign Secretary replied – and passed on.

It was difficult to remember each individual in such a sea of faces as one Statesman succeeded another.

After them came the Diplomatic Corps.

"His Excellency, Don Alfonso Gerona, the Spanish Ambassador, and Madame Gerona!"

Anastasia looked at them with interest.

They gave her their good wishes, speaking in Spanish, and she replied in the same language.

She had a feeling that the King turned for a moment to look at her in approval, and then Comte Henri le Granmont, Ambassador of His Imperial Majesty, the

Emperor of France and the Comtesse le Granmont took their place.

Anastasia was suddenly alert.

She remembered what Christopher Lyncombe had said and, even while she was curtsying to the French Ambassador, out of the corner of her eye she glanced at his wife.

She saw an exquisitely-gowned woman curtsying almost over-effusively to the King and realised as she did so that two dark eyes looked up at him from under long lashes with a provocative expression in them that was inescapable.

It would not have been noticeable, Anastasia told herself, if she had not been looking out for just such a sign of intimacy between the Comtesse and her future husband.

The King's voice was, however, quite formal and unemotional, although there was undoubtedly a caressing note in the Comtesse's voice as she spoke to him.

Then, as the French Ambassador moved away and the Comtesse curtseyed to Anastasia, there was no mistaking the change in her expression and the sudden hardness in her eyes.

"I must bid you welcome to Maurona, ma'am," the Comtesse said, and Anastasia thought wryly that there was certainly no welcome in her tone.

"I am so delighted to meet you, *madame*," Anastasia replied in perfect French. "I have heard so much about you."

She saw the sudden surprise in the Comtesse's face, but before she could think of an adequate answer

Anastasia turned to the Italian Ambassador who had just shaken hands with the King.

The procession went on and on until, when at last it finished, the King once again offered Anastasia his arm and they mingled with the guests who were now drinking wine and eating refreshments in the room adjoining the Throne Room.

They spoke first to one person and then another, while Captain Carlos Aznar hovered near them.

Then Anastasia saw the Comtesse le Granmont deliberately walk forward so that it was impossible for the King to proceed without speaking to her.

The Comtesse curtsied.

"We are hoping, Your Majesty, that it will be possible for you to bring Her Royal Highness to the reception at the French Embassy this afternoon. It would be so delightful if you would watch the procession through the streets from our balconies from which there is a much better view than from the Chancellery."

The Comtesse was looking at the King as she spoke, but Anastasia, watching her, had the feeling there was something more behind her words.

Then she was sure that this was yet another attempt to inveigle the King into showing his affection for the French community.

Before he could answer, Anastasia parried,

"It sounds delightful, *madame*, but I have the feeling that, as it will be my first appearance in public, I should stand on Mauronian soil."

She smiled as she spoke and added,

"I may be mistaken, but I am sure I have read somewhere that an Embassy not only represents but is a piece of its own country. Therefore in the French Embassy I should in effect be in France."

It would have been difficult for anyone to suspect her of being anything but ingenuous.

Nevertheless, the Comtesse's face darkened.

Pointedly she ignored Anastasia.

"I am hoping you will not refuse our invitation, Sire," she carried on in a soft voice.

"I think the decision must be in the hands of my future bride," the King answered. "She may, indeed, be too fatigued to fulfil any more engagements. She has had a most exhausting journey."

"Perhaps we could talk about it a little later," Anastasia suggested. "I would so much like to see the procession and the Battle of Flowers."

Again she spoke ingenuously, but the Comtesse's lips were set in a hard line as Anastasia and the King moved away.

Anastasia glanced at Captain Aznar.

He had heard the whole conversation and she saw that he could not hide the delight in his expression.

She had the feeling that the King was looking at her rather speculatively as if he suspected there might be some particular reason for her elusiveness in the face of the Comtesse's insistence.

There were still a large number of people to meet, but at last, when Anastasia was now feeling extremely hungry, the King drew her away from the reception room and they walked down the corridor towards another part of the Palace.

"I think it is time for luncheon," he said, "and may I congratulate you? You came through your first ordeal with flying colours."

"Did I really?" Anastasia asked. "Everyone was so charming. I only wish I could believe all the nice words they said."

"Why not?" he asked. "And have I been so remiss as not to inform you that you are very lovely – far more beautiful than I could have possibly have expected?"

She knew he was echoing her first words to him and she blushed as she said,

"I am so ashamed that I should have spoken like that without thinking."

"Do you often do that?"

"Nearly always!" she confessed. "You looked so absolutely different from what I had anticipated that I could not believe it was true."

"And what do you think I look like now?" he enquired.

She looked up at him from under the brim of her bonnet.

Never had she seen a more attractive face. His features were classical, just as they had appeared in the portrait in the *Illustrated London News*. His nose might have been Roman or Greek and his broad forehead might have come from the same source.

But his eyes were definitely raffish – the eyes of a pirate or an adventurer, a man who looked at the world with curiosity and a desire for plunder! There was also a twist to his lips that was decidedly mocking.

He did not look like anyone she had ever seen before and yet, she told herself, with his broad shoulders and narrow, athletic figure he was very masculine and extremely attractive.

"Well?" the King asked breaking in on her thoughts. "I am waiting and, let me add, I am extremely apprehensive!"

"You need not be," Anastasia said, "I think you look just as a King should look. Was Alexander one of your ancestors?"

"The Great?" the King queried. "Are you expecting me to conquer the world?"

"I think 'the world' means something different for each one of us," Anastasia answered. "It could be just a home and garden – or half a continent."

She paused and added,

"And sometimes it is a case of conquer or be conquered."

She saw the astonishment in the King's eyes, but before he could reply they had reached the State Banqueting Hall.

Chapter Five

"You are nearly ready now, so I will go and put on my tiara," the Grand Duchess announced.

Anastasia was unable to answer as, at that moment, Olivia lifted her wedding dress over her head. Only when the huge full skirt was pulled over its whalebone frame and she slipped her arms into a small tight bodice, was she able to reply,

"Yes, do, Mama. I don't want to be a late bride."

"You certainly do not wish to be early!" the Grand Duchess retorted, as if she must always have the last word. She went from the room and Anastasia stood still while Olivia buttoned up her gown at the back.

She could see herself reflected in a long mirror and she knew that the wedding dress she and her mother had chosen with such care justified the exorbitant amount of money it had cost.

The satin bodice was embroidered all over with diamante, and the full skirt, trimmed with three flounces of Honiton lace and sprays of orange flowers and myrtle, sparkled with diamante like dew drops on a flower.

There were more orange flowers just below the curve of Anastasia's white shoulders, and the long train, which was to be affixed at the last moment, was lying on the bed.

Edged with ermine and also embroidered in diamante, it was very impressive. Anastasia hoped that the four pages that were to carry it would be able to sustain its weight, for she reckoned it would be very heavy.

"You look lovely, Your Royal Highness!" Olivia murmured.

For a moment they were alone in the room, as the other maid, who had been assisting Anastasia to dress, had gone to fetch the bouquet.

"I hope all the people waiting outside will think so," Anastasia replied.

"Already they are talking of you as the Queen they longed for!" Olivia answered. "The whole city is gossiping of how you added the red carnations to your bouquet yesterday afternoon."

Anastasia smiled.

She was glad to think she had avoided an awkward situation – or had it been a trap?

She and the King, her mother and a great number of officials had arrived at the Chancellery to watch the procession of flowers.

Anastasia, half afraid that the King might be annoyed that she had refused the invitation of the Comtesse to the French Embassy, was making every effort to be charming and enthusiastic.

She hoped that the King would not think she was suspicious of the French Ambassadress, or that her explanation that she must watch the procession on Mauronian soil had a deeper motive than had appeared on the surface.

She had known, however, that Captain Aznar was delighted with what she had said, and she could not help feeling that her action would lose nothing in the telling.

She considered whether she would tell him not to speak of it, but there was no possibility of her having a private conversation with him.

After they had lunched formally in the huge State Banqueting Hall, there was only time for Anastasia to go upstairs and rest for half an hour before she changed ready to proceed with the King to the Chancellery.

The Grand Duchess had thought it wise for Anastasia to wear a predominantly white dress to make her appearance on the balcony.

"They will expect you to look like a bride," she insisted.

The gown she had chosen was very attractive. It was white, trimmed with tiny flouncings over the full skirt. Each flounce was threaded through with pale pink ribbon, and the same ribbons decorated Anastasia's small bonnet, which tied under her chin.

She looked very young and very lovely as she came down the stairs of the Palace to where the King, surrounded by Courtiers, *aides-de-camp* and resplendent officials, stood waiting for her.

He raised her hand to his lips and she could not put a name to the expression she saw in his eyes.

She hoped it was admiration, but she was not sure.

She thought a trifle unhappily that there was definitely a mocking twist to his lips.

"Are you always so punctual?" he asked, as they walked down the red-carpeted steps of the Palace to where the carriages were waiting. "I had anticipated I might have to wait for my future bride – and certainly for my wife!"

"Doubtless tapping the floor impatiently with your foot!" Anastasia laughed. "I shall be very careful in case Your Majesty begins to stamp. That is when it is really dangerous!"

"You speak as if you had some experience of impatient men," the King commented.

"Mama has told me how cross my father used to become if anyone kept him waiting," Anastasia answered, "with the result that I am always afraid of being over punctual and finding that there is no one to receive me!"

They reached the carriage, and once they had started on their way it was impossible to talk because of the cheers of the crowd.

It was only a short distance to the Chancellery, but Anastasia found it exhilarating to hear the cries ring out, to find the carriage filling with flowers as it had on her way from the battleship and to see that many people were carrying a picture of her, holding it up on hastily, improvised banners or fixed to pieces of wood.

There was also a profusion of Union Jacks mingling with the flags of Maurona.

"Do you always get such an enthusiastic reception in your Capital?" Anastasia asked the King.

"Very seldom," he replied. "It is *you* they are cheering."

"Not me alone," Anastasia replied, "but us, because we are together."

She thought for a moment he was about to say something cynical.

Instead he smiled and said, again with that mocking note in his voice,

"You say all the right things. I cannot help thinking you have been extremely well trained!"

"That is not very flattering," Anastasia said severely. "It makes me sound like a performing bear!"

The King laughed, and she knew that he was surprised to find she was so quick-witted.

They were received with much pomp at the door of the Chancellery and were escorted up through a rather ancient and gloomy building to the Council Chamber. Off this was the balcony from which they were to view the procession.

As they were being received, a child, obviously the daughter of one of the officials, handed Anastasia a bouquet. She accepted it, said a few words to the child and, carrying it in her hand, proceeded up the stairs.

There were more introductions in the Council Chamber, most of them to wives of officials, and then, as flunkeys went forward to open the long windows to the balcony, Anastasia heard Captain Aznar's voice beside her.

"White carnations," he said barely above a whisper, "are worn by the French element in Maurona, red by the Spanish."

For the first time Anastasia looked closely at her bouquet. She had noticed as the child presented it to her that it was white. Now she saw that it was composed entirely of white carnations.

She wondered if she should leave it on a table in the Council Chamber. Then she thought that if she did so, some officious courtier was sure to think it was an oversight and put it back into her hands.

She looked around the assembled company and saw that more of the ladies were carrying bouquets. Then she realised that there were magnificent arrangements of flowers on side tables around the room.

She walked towards the nearest.

"How beautiful your flowers are!" she exclaimed at large to those standing around her. "I cannot tell you what a joy they are to someone who has come from the cold and snows of England."

Reaching the table she smiled at a lady at her side and said,

"I am so looking forward to visiting your perfume factory. I have been told of the delicious fragrance of those perfumes distilled in Sergei."

"We hope very much that you will like them, ma'am," the lady replied.

A woman of little importance, she was overcome to find herself talking intimately with the Princess.

Anastasia looked again at the floral display in front of her. She saw what she was seeking! The base of the arrangement was composed almost entirely of red carnations.

"I wonder," she said in almost conspiratorial tones to the woman to whom she had been talking, "if I might take some of these beautiful red carnations? They have such a delightful fragrance."

She did not wait for an answer, but picked up a whole handful of the carnations from the table and put them against the white flowers of her bouquet.

"Is not that pretty?" she exclaimed again in that ingenuous voice that made her actions seem natural and unpremeditated.

"It is indeed very pretty, ma'am," another lady remarked who was standing near, "and we are all delighted that you find our flowers so attractive."

"They are as beautiful as your country," Anastasia said, "and it would be difficult to say anything more appreciative."

The windows that led to the balcony were now opened and Anastasia turned towards them to join the King, who had not followed her when she had moved across the room to admire the flowers.

He glanced at the red and white bouquet she now held in her hand and, if he understood the significance of her action, he did not show it. But there was no doubt that the gesture was not wasted on the crowd outside.

As Anastasia stepped on to the small platform that had been erected on the balcony to hold the two chairs for her and the King, a roar went up from the crowd.

For a moment it seemed the usual full-throated acclamation they had received all along the route from the Palace. Then, as if by magic, scarlet appeared everywhere, scarlet flags, scarlet handkerchiefs, ties and pieces of bunting were being waved and those who were waving them appeared to shout more noisily and more vivaciously than the rest of the crowd.

Anastasia and the King waved in response to the acclamation, and almost as soon as they were on the balcony the procession started to pass below them.

There were carts and carriages of every sort and description, drays and floats drawn by men instead of horses. On them were beautiful girls dressed to represent traditional characters of Mauronian and Mediterranean history.

There were arches and huge shells, stars and hearts, all made of flowers, and following the procession were more carriages filled with men and women in fancy dress for the battle.

Flowers were thrown from the carriages and flowers were thrown by the crowd at the procession and at each other. The air seemed to be full of blossoms and Anastasia could smell their fragrance.

It was all very gay, although occasionally there were scuffles in the crowd as someone who had been hit too hard in the face retaliated by throwing something heavier and more dangerous than a posy of flowers.

But on the whole it was extremely good tempered and, when Anastasia said goodbye at the Chancellery door, she said with a sincerity it was impossible to doubt,

"It has been more amusing and more fun than I can possibly express."

"You enjoyed yourself?" the King asked as they drove back towards the Palace.

"I am so sorry that I shall have to wait another year before I can see another Battle of Flowers," she said. "What will the people do tonight?"

"There will be dancing, drinking and fireworks," the King answered.

Anastasia sighed.

"It sounds wonderful! I wish we could go and dance."

"I am afraid that would be impossible."

"Supposing we wore fancy dress and were masked?" Anastasia suggested.

"I cannot think your mother would consider it a good idea."

"I am afraid you are right," Anastasia agreed reluctantly. "Why do ordinary people have so much more fun than we do?"

"I wonder if they do?" the King answered. "Most of the year they have to work very hard."

"As we must also, if we are to do our job properly," Anastasia replied.

"And what work do you intend to do," he asked, "apart from conventional engagements, such as the opening of a Town Hall or visiting a hospital?"

She had a feeling that he was deliberately mocking her and she answered,

"I cannot believe there are not a great many more things to do than that, but first I must get to know your people and understand them."

"Do you think that will be easy?" the King asked.

"Why not? I have a feeling that people you find everywhere and in every class or circumstance are very much the same underneath. They all have their worries and their difficulties – they all want happiness."

They were nearing the Palace and the King turned towards her in the carriage to say,

"You are very different from what I expected."

"What *did* you expect?" Anastasia asked. "Someone aloof, autocratic and empty-headed?"

She remembered what the Prime Minister had said and added,

"And, of course, with protruding teeth!"

The King laughed.

"Shall I tell you that your teeth are like pearls?"

"It sounds rather like a phrase in the novelettes Mama will not allow me to read," she said. "But if it is meant as a compliment, then I accept it with pleasure."

"You must have received plenty of compliments in England," the King suggested.

"Not many," Anastasia answered, "so I am extremely greedy where they are concerned."

Again the King laughed and then they reached the Palace and there was no more chance of private conversation.

Anastasia found that because she was to be married the following day she was not allowed to dine with the King but was to eat alone with her mother.

The Grand Duchess took the opportunity of lecturing her at some length on her duty as regards her future subjects and her behaviour in general.

"Do try to behave in a more circumspect manner, Anastasia," she begged. "You know how impulsive you are and how you say whatever comes into your head without a thought for the consequences. That is not what is expected of a Royal Sovereign."

"I will try to think before I speak, Mama."

But while answering her mother, she was thinking actually of the Comtesse le Granmont, and wondering whether the King would see her during the evening.

She could not help feeling depressed because the Comtesse was so very attractive and her looks were so obviously a complete contrast to her own.

She felt she could understand a man finding those dark expressive eyes alluring and the red pouting lips very inviting.

Anastasia thought of the King kissing them and felt in a sudden panic that her marriage was already a failure. What, compared to the Comtesse, had she to offer a man so experienced, so handsome, or indeed so raffish?

The King and the Comtesse were, she thought, complementary to each other – both of them sophisticated, a man and a woman of the world, while she was only an ignorant girl who knew nothing and had seen little beyond the confines of Hampton Court Palace.

She had a sudden impulse to fling her arms round her mother and beg for her help and guidance.

But she knew the Grand Duchess would not understand and would in fact merely reiterate what she had already said.

'All I have been told,' Anastasia thought, 'is that it is my duty to obey the King, and to shut my eyes to anything which I am not expected to see.'

She could not help remembering the manner in which the Comtesse had looked up at King Maximilian and the caressing note in her voice when she had spoken to him.

'*She loves him and he loves her*!' Anastasia was convinced, and felt her heart sink dismally at the idea.

Now, as she moved towards the dressing table to sit down so that Olivia could arrange her veil and headdress, she said involuntarily,

"I feel as if I am in a dream and this cannot really be happening to me!"

Olivia picked up the beautiful wreath that Anastasia was to wear on her head.

It was fashioned of diamonds in the shape of flowers and so skilfully and cleverly contrived that the flowers and leaves moved a little with the wearer so that they almost looked as if they were alive.

Then Olivia looked over her shoulder as if to make sure there was no one else in the room before she said in a low voice,

"I have something to tell Your Royal Highness."

Anastasia was suddenly alert.

"What is it?" she asked.

"I have not told Your Royal Highness before, but the young man I am to marry is employed at the French Embassy."

Anastasia did not reply, but she raised her eyes to the maid's face.

"When I left for England, Your Royal Highness, Pedro was second valet to His Excellency the French Ambassador. While I was away he was promoted and he is now First Valet."

Still Anastasia waited.

"He went with His Excellency to Marseilles," Olivia went on, "from where he has just returned. There were meetings – secret meetings with officials who had come from Paris."

"Does Pedro know what these meetings were about?" Anastasia enquired.

"No, Your Royal Highness, but he suspected they deeply concerned our country."

"Why should he suspect that?"

"There are things that he has heard in the last month or so, trifling in themselves, and yet Pedro is sure that they indicate a danger to Maurona."

"What do you think might happen?"

Olivia drew in her breath.

"The French wish to annex Maurona, Your Royal Highness. Pedro is sure of it!"

Anastasia turned to look at herself in the mirror.

She could see her own face, white and serious, and behind her Olivia's anxious, worried eyes.

"We shall have to be absolutely sure," Anastasia remarked after a moment.

"Of course, Your Royal Highness, Pedro knows that, but he is convinced that nothing will occur before the British ship which brought you here leaves the harbour."

"That is tonight!" Anastasia said, as if she spoke to herself.

"Tonight?" Olivia echoed.

"Yes," Anastasia replied. "The Grand Duchess will leave immediately after the wedding. The ship's Captain is not satisfied with the repairs carried out in Gibraltar. He wants to put in at Marseilles, and it has been arranged for the Grand Duchess to travel that far in the *Warrior* and then take a train across France."

Olivia did not reply and Anastasia said,

"Ask your young man if he learns any more to let you know at once."

As she spoke, she wondered wildly what she could do if Pedro's information was alarming. Then she thought of Captain Aznar and knew that he would help her.

"There is one thing more, Your Royal Highness," Olivia said, "although I do not know if I should speak of it."

"You know that anything which concerns the future of your country is of importance and interest to me. As I asked you to do when we were aboard the *Warrior*, please tell me everything you know."

Olivia looked down nervously at the wreath she held in her hands.

"It is just, that Pedro has been told by the servants in the Embassy, that the Comtesse le Granmont has been coming to the Palace at night to be alone with His Majesty!"

Anastasia drew in her breath.

"Where do they meet?"

"In His Majesty's private room. It can be reached through the garden by a door at the side of the Palace, which is used by no one else. There is also a door in the garden wall through which the Comtesse enters – and only the King has a key to it."

"Thank you for telling me," Anastasia said in a quiet, unemotional voice. "I hope, Olivia, you are in constant touch with your young man and that you will see him after the wedding."

"I shall try to do so, Your Royal Highness," Olivia answered, "but – "

Whatever she was about to add was left unsaid, for at that moment the Grand Duchess wafted into the bedroom.

"Are you not ready, Anastasia?" she asked sharply. "Time is getting on. You should be dressed by now."

"There is only my wreath and veil, Mama," Anastasia replied.

She had chosen to wear off the face a Honiton lace veil such as the Queen's elder daughter, the Princess Royal, had worn on her marriage to Prince Frederick of Prussia.

It was very becoming, and the sparkling diamonds on Anastasia's fair hair made her look like a star twinkling in the evening sky.

She put on her lace gloves that fastened at the wrist, picked up the bouquet, which had been brought to her room, and noted with relief that it was fashioned not of carnations but of white orchids.

Finally, when her long train was fixed to her shoulders, the pages were brought into the bedroom to lift it up and carry it carefully as they followed Anastasia and the Grand Duchess down the wide staircase towards the hall of the Palace.

As Anastasia had no father to give her away, Sir Frederick Falkland, the British Ambassador, was to escort her up the aisle.

The Grand Duchess went ahead of them in a closed carriage, and Anastasia and Sir Frederick were in a magnificent coach emblazoned with the Royal Crown.

The coach had particularly large glass windows on either side of it so that the crowds could see her.

It was drawn by four white horses and followed by a squadron of the Mauronian Cavalry. In their dashing helmets with plumed feathers floating in the breeze, their polished breastplates and high boots, they looked magnificent.

The whole entourage, Anastasia could not help thinking, really looked as if it had stepped out of an illustrated storybook.

The route was lined with soldiers and the crowds seemed even greater than they had before.

Everywhere there was a profusion of Union Jacks, which caused the British Ambassador to remark,

"Your reception is very gratifying, ma'am, and it is obvious the Mauronians have a partiality for the British. I know that Her Majesty the Queen will be delighted with the report I shall be sending her about the enthusiasm of the populace."

"They seem to be a happy people," Anastasia replied. "Let us hope they remain so."

"That may depend upon you, ma'am," the Ambassador remarked.

"I hope I shall have a chance to get to know the people before anything occurs," Anastasia answered.

She spoke without thinking.

"What do you think might occur?" Sir Frederick asked sharply. "Has anyone suggested there might be trouble?"

Anastasia was sorry she had spoken. This was not the moment, she thought, to tell Sir Frederick of her fears, and besides, she had the feeling he would be little or no help if there was a confrontation with the French.

She knew Sir Frederick was waiting for her answer and she replied evasively,

"There seems to be trouble in so many countries, Sir Frederick, even our own, that I was just hoping that everything would run smoothly here, until I have had time to settle down, so to speak."

"Yes, of course, I can understand that, ma'am," Sir Frederick replied, and Anastasia was careful not to say anything else controversial before they reached the Cathedral.

The cheering was so loud as she stepped from the carriage to find her four pages waiting for her, that it was hard to hear the Church bells pealing above the noise.

But in contrast to the cheers and the sunshine the Cathedral itself seemed quiet and solemn.

The pages arranged themselves on each side of her train, and because she had no friends in Maurona there were no bridesmaids, only one Matron-of-Honour, the daughter of the Prime Minister.

She was a pretty dark girl who looked very attractive in a dress of rose pink, carrying a bouquet of the special roses from which the perfume of Sergei was distilled.

Slowly Anastasia moved up the aisle preceded by the Archbishop who had greeted her at the door and a number of the clergy in magnificently embroidered vestments.

As she passed the guests, the women swept to the ground in a curtsy, but on her mother's instructions Anastasia kept her head bowed.

Only when she reached the Chancel did she look from under her eyelashes at the Royalty who were seated on either side in pews that on other occasions accommodated the choir and cathedral clergy.

She had already seen a list of those who were to be present and had found there was no one whom she had met before at Windsor Castle.

None of them looked particularly interesting and she found herself wishing she had just one or two relatives of her own who could have been there on this, the most important day of her life.

Then ahead, at the altar steps, she saw the King.

He was looking even more resplendent than he had yesterday on her arrival.

He was wearing full dress military uniform, and it became him so well that Anastasia found herself thinking he was not only the most attractive but also quite the most handsome man she had ever seen.

Then she remembered that the Comtesse le Granmont would be watching him and perhaps he would be thinking of her.

As they knelt side by side and the Archbishop blessed them, Anastasia prayed,

'Please God – help me to make the King happy – it will not be easy – but I will try to be good – so help me – please, please help me!'

In the State Coach, which conveyed them very slowly from the Cathedral to the Palace, the King said as their hands moved automatically to acknowledge the cheering crowds,

"One blessing, Anastasia, is that we shall never have to go through this again!"

"Are you not enjoying yourself?" Anastasia asked him in consternation.

"If you want the truth, I find such pomp and circumstance extremely boring," the King answered.

"I am – sorry," Anastasia murmured uncertainly.

"Why should you be? I was wrong to complain! Our wedding day should be an ecstatic occasion!"

His voice was mocking and cynical.

Then, as he saw her expression, he put out his free hand and found hers.

"Forgive me," he said gently in a very different tone. "I want you to be happy and sometimes I forget how young you are and that this is all new to you and doubtless exciting."

"I do find it very – exciting," Anastasia answered.

She was not certain if it was the ceremony she had in mind, or the feeling of his hand on hers.

*

The banquet that was waiting for them when they arrived back at the Palace seemed to go on endlessly. Course succeeded course and the crystal glasses beside everyone's plate were filled to the brim with superlative wines.

Anastasia began to feel a little tired. The diamond wreath was heavy on her head and the State Banqueting Hall with so many people in it seemed stifling.

At the same time she knew she must make every effort to create a good impression on the royal personages who had come so far for the wedding ceremony.

In fact it was easy to charm the men, but she had a feeling that the Queens and Princesses looked at her a little contemptuously, as if they thought her far too immature to take her place among them.

But perhaps it was only her imagination, and maybe she was feeling particularly sensitive during an ordeal, which was more demanding than anything she had ever been obliged to experience before.

There were long speeches, all in French, and finally the King himself rose to reply to them.

Anastasia was glad that he spoke briefly and managed to make the assembled company laugh.

He said how much he welcomed their company on what was undoubtedly the happiest day of his life, on which he had been married to someone so beautiful and so charming that it was difficult to believe there was another man in the whole world who could have been more blessed by fate.

'He does not mean a word of it,' Anastasia thought to herself.

Relentlessly her eyes were drawn to where, at another table, the diplomatic representatives of many countries were seated.

She could see the Comtesse le Granmont, it would indeed have been impossible not to notice her, however large the crowd.

She was wearing a dress of emerald green that seemed more voluminous, more ostentatious and more elaborately contrived than the gown of any other woman in the room. Her tiara was certainly higher and, more impressive than those of the other diplomats' wives, and the emeralds and diamonds round her neck and wrists almost outshone the crystal chandeliers.

But it was not her clothes that made Anastasia keep glancing at her, but the attractiveness of her face.

'She is fascinating,' Anastasia thought dismally, 'in a manner that I could never hope to emulate!'

She could see the Comtesse gesticulating, her eyes flashing as she talked, and she realised that even the other diplomats, familiar as they must be with her, were apparently entranced by what she had to say.

She wondered if the King was watching her too, and while she did not actually see him glance in her direction, she could not help feeling that he could not fail to notice anyone so obviously outstanding, even if he had not been wishing to see her for other reasons.

When the banquet was over, there was a reception in the Hall of Mirrors to which a great many other guests had been invited.

Here a six-tiered wedding cake was waiting to be cut and powdered flunkeys were dispensing champagne.

A band was playing softly in one corner of the Hall and once again, despite the crowds, Anastasia could see herself reflected and re-reflected in the mirrors that lined the walls.

There were so many people to talk to and a bewildering sea of faces moved before her eyes, and yet none had substance.

Captain Aznar brought Anastasia a glass of champagne.

"I feel you need it, ma'am."

"Thank you," Anastasia answered gratefully.

Three times during the reception Anastasia and the King had to go out on the balcony of the Palace to wave to the great crowds of people assembled outside.

A roar of voices greeted them and the sound was deafening as they stood looking down at their enthusiastic and rejoicing subjects.

Then, after the reception had seemed to go on for hours and hours, Anastasia had to say goodbye to her mother. The Grand Duchess, fortunately, was not travelling alone, for there were several European Royalties who were glad of the chance to get home quickly by travelling in *H.M.S. Warrior* rather than overland.

"Goodbye, dearest Mama," Anastasia said wistfully and wanted to ask her to stay.

"Goodbye, my dear child," the Grand Duchess replied. "This has been a very happy day for me. I only wish your father could have been here to see you married and to meet your husband."

"I am sure he would have been pleased, Mama."

The Grand Duchess and her companions left from a side door of the Palace to avoid the crowds, and Anastasia and the King stood waving until the carriage had turned out of the gate.

It was as they walked back towards the hall that Anastasia suddenly felt alone.

It was as if her last link with England had gone and now she had no one to depend upon, no one to guide her, except perhaps her husband.

She glanced a little nervously at the King.

"Are you tired?" he asked. "Would you like to retire? I am afraid I have a large number of relatives to whom I must say goodbye before I can consider myself 'off duty'."

"If no one would think it rude, I would like a chance to take off my wreath, which is very heavy."

"How stupid of me!" the King exclaimed. "I should have remembered that my mother always said it gave her a headache. You could have perhaps changed into something lighter."

"It is too late now," Anastasia said with a smile, "but if you are certain no one will miss me, I would like to go upstairs."

"I will come to you as soon as I can," the King said. "Thank you, Anastasia for having been so charming to everyone."

He raised her hands to his lips, and Anastasia found that Captain Aznar was at her side waiting to escort her upstairs.

They moved out of earshot of the servants before she asked,

"Was everything all right?"

"You know it was, ma'am! You were absolutely amazing! They went up several steps before he said,

"Your gesture with your bouquet yesterday has caught the imagination of the people. The newspapers are full of it."

"I am afraid I have not had time to look at them," Anastasia said.

"That is not surprising," he replied. "But you have made our people think you care about them, and that is exactly what I prayed you would do."

"I owe so much to you," Anastasia said.

She saw the pleasure in his eyes, and then she bade him goodnight and went into her bedroom.

Olivia was waiting for her.

Anastasia sat down thankfully on a chair and let her maid take the wreath from her head. As she did so she looked at a small gold clock on her dressing table and realised it was later than she had expected.

"Does Your Majesty want anything to eat or drink?" Olivia asked.

Anastasia shook her head.

"I could not face anything more," she answered. "I thought the banquet would never end!"

"They are always protracted," Olivia answered, "but when His Majesty is alone he eats very quickly and only has a small number of courses."

"That is something to be grateful for!"

"Would you like to go to bed, Your Majesty?" Olivia enquired.

"I think I will undress," Anastasia answered. "Very few guests have left and I feel it will be a long time before the King gets away."

"I should think it will be an hour or more. Your Majesty has had a very tiring day, but you looked beautiful, more beautiful than any Queen of Maurona has ever looked!"

Anastasia had a bath and then Olivia handed her one of the beautiful nightgowns, which she and the Grand Duchess had bought in Bond Street.

It was inset with lace and over it Anastasia put on a wrapper of pale blue satin, the wide sleeves of which were edged with swansdown. It was a diaphanous garment that seemed to encompass her like a blue cloud. With her fair hair and big blue eyes, she looked rather like a small angel fallen out of a summer sky.

It was after half past eleven when Olivia left her, but Anastasia did not get into bed. Instead she sat down in a deep armchair by the fireside.

It had been warm during the day, but now the sun had gone down there was a chill in the air from the mountain snow, which still lingered on the distant peaks.

She sat staring into the flames and the clock on the mantelpiece chimed midnight before the door, which communicated with the King's Suite opened, and the King came in.

He too had undressed and was wearing a long robe to the floor with a high velvet collar and deep cuffs. He closed the door behind him and advanced towards the hearthrug.

"Not in bed, Anastasia?" he asked. "I thought you would be tired after such a long day."

"I am tired," Anastasia answered, "but I want to – talk to – you."

The King smiled.

"Is it not rather late for conversation?"

"Not for what I – have to – say," Anastasia answered.

He looked at her and she thought there was a searching glance in his eyes as if she perplexed him.

Then, because she obviously expected it of him, he sat down in the chair opposite her.

The firelight played on Anastasia's hair turning it to living gold and illuminating her small, serious face.

The only other light in the room came from the candles and candelabra standing on either side of the big canopied and silk-draped bed.

"We have not had a chance to be alone until now," the King said, as Anastasia did not speak. "I am sorry that the storm should have delayed you so that we had no opportunity to get to know each other before we were married."

He paused and added,

"May I say how very happy I am that you should be my wife? I have a feeling, Anastasia, that we have many years of contentment ahead of us."

Anastasia drew in her breath and then she murmured in a very small voice,

"You will not be – angry if tell you what I am – thinking?"

"I am sure I would find it very difficult to be angry with you."

"You cannot be certain of that until you – hear what I have to – say."

"I cannot imagine what it is you want to tell me," he said, "but if it will make things any easier for you, I am prepared to promise I will not be angry."

Anastasia looked at him, her eyes very blue in the light from the flames.

"I – think," she said in a hesitating little voice, "that you will – expect tonight – now that we are – married, a- and other people will expect it too, that, you – should make – love to me."

"It is certainly usual where a bride and groom are concerned."

"I do not – know, because Mama would not – tell me," Anastasia went on, "what – happens when a man makes love to his – wife, but for us – I think it would be a – mistake."

There was no doubt that the King was surprised.

He had been leaning back in the armchair looking at Anastasia and now he sat up and for a moment there was no smile on his lips.

"Why should you think it a mistake?" he asked.

"Because," Anastasia replied, "if two people are to – make love together – they should be in – love."

The King was still and then he said,

"We have had no opportunity, Anastasia, of falling in love with each other."

"I – I know that," Anastasia answered, "and – because I think you – love someone else, I would not – want you to – pretend where I am concerned."

The King stiffened.

"Who has been talking to you?" he asked sharply.

Anastasia did not reply and he said,

"If I thought it was one of my servants – Captain Aznar, for instance – I would dismiss him instantly!"

"No – no, Captain Aznar would not presume to mention such a thing," Anastasia answered. "I was told that your heart was – involved before I left England."

"Surely that is impossible!" the King ejaculated. "Who could have dared to suggest – who could have known?"

"That is immaterial. The point is I do know that you – care for someone."

"And yet you were prepared to marry me?" the King asked.

"I had no choice – at least, that is not quite true – "

"There was someone else who wished to marry you?"

"Yes, there was," Anastasia admitted, "but it would not have been permitted and we should have had to run away."

"And you were not brave enough to do so?"

There was no mistaking the cynical twist to his lips.

"It was not that," Anastasia replied. "If I had loved him enough I would have gone, however – reprehensible it might have been, however angry it would have made Mama and the Queen – but I did not love him."

"But he loved you?"

"Yes."

"Were you not tempted, in the circumstances, to go away with a man who loved you rather than come to a strange country to marry a man whom you thought cared for someone else?"

"I did think about it very seriously," Anastasia answered, "but when I was sure I did not love Christopher, I thought it would be stupid to cause such a fuss."

"Are you quite certain you do not love him?" the King asked curiously.

"When he tried to kiss me I – struggled because I did not – want him to," Anastasia explained.

"You have never been kissed?"

Anastasia shook her head.

"No, and that is why I feel I would not want you to kiss me when you were wishing that you were – kissing – someone else."

"It would not be like that," the King said in his deep voice. "I would like to kiss you, Anastasia, and I would not be thinking of anyone else."

"You could not be sure of that," Anastasia replied, "and certainly I would be – thinking of – *her*."

The King rose to his feet as if he found it difficult to think when he was sitting down.

He walked across the big room to the bed and back again.

"I will be frank with you, Anastasia," he said after a moment. "I never expected to have a conversation like this with you on our wedding night. I understand – of course I understand –what you have been trying to say to me, but I think it important that we should live what might be called a 'normal' married life."

He paused before he continued,

"If I *'make love'* to you, as you call it, I would not be thinking of anyone else. I would be thinking of you and I hope you will find that we will enjoy together what can be a very happy and fulfilling experience."

Anastasia looked at him her eyes very wide and then she said,

"I am very – ignorant of such matters, but I have been – told about the beautiful – ladies of Paris, and how gentlemen like yourself and the – Emperor visit them and give them magnificent presents – "

She paused and after a moment the King responded curiously,

"Go on!"

"I don't understand what – happens, or why the ladies are – paid so extravagantly, but I have been thinking – perhaps incorrectly – that the only – difference between what they give a man and what I could – give him would be – love."

The King sat silent, suddenly still, almost as if he had been arrested.

"You may laugh at me for thinking this," Anastasia continued after a moment in a worried little voice, "but surely the actual – love-making between a man and a woman must have been the same all through the ages since – Adam and Eve?"

The King did not answer and she went on,

"That is why the difference – I have thought – must be not in a person's body, but in their mind. Am I – wrong?"

She waited anxiously while her question seemed to hang in the air between them.

Then the King said very quietly,

"No, Anastasia. You are right! But I am surprised that you should have worked it out for yourself."

"I thought how love has inspired so many people in the past," Anastasia answered. "I thought of Helen of Troy – of the knights who fought for their ladies' favours and were prepared to die so that they would be proud of them."

She made a nervous little gesture with her hand as she carried on,

"I thought of Romeo and Juliet, Dante and Beatrice, and other famous lovers and I am certain that what is important, what one should always search for if one is to have a happy marriage, is – love."

The King's eyes were on her face and she continued,

"Please don't be angry – but you do understand that I am asking you not to – really be my – husband until perhaps we can come to – love each other."

"I am certainly not angry," the King replied after a moment, "I am just surprised!"

"I want to be a very good Queen," Anastasia said earnestly, "and I would like to be a good wife as well – and I think it might be easy – when I get to know you better – to fall in love with you."

She gave a little sigh,

"But perhaps you will never be in love with me."

There was a long silence.

"I think the only answer to that," the King said eventually, "is that we shall have to wait and see. You have explained everything very sensibly and intelligently, Anastasia. In describing to me your attractions before you arrived in Maurona, they forgot to mention that you have an extremely astute brain. It was something I had not anticipated."

"It is kind of you not to be – angry."

"I deeply regret that you should have heard rumours about my indiscretions before you had even arrived. That is something that should not have occurred."

Anastasia smiled.

"Everyone talks about Kings! I doubt, however hard you tried – if it would have been possible for you to keep your love affairs completely private."

The King looked startled.

"Are you saying that everything I do is common knowledge?"

"I am not suggesting that everyone knows for certain," Anastasia replied, "but people talk, they gossip. Even though it hardly seems possible, scandals are related from one country to another by those who love to tittle-tattle about famous people, especially when they are handsome Monarchs."

She was thinking of Lady Walters as she spoke and the King laughed a little ruefully,

"I see I have underestimated my own importance. It is something people have seldom accused me of doing in the past!"

He was silent for a moment and then he reflected,

"Taking into account what you have just said to me, Anastasia, I think we have both to face the fact that anything we do now will be gossiped about and certainly noticed in Maurona."

"Yes, of course," Anastasia agreed.

"And that is why for me to accede to what you have suggested, to leave your room at this moment and sleep in my own bed, would doubtless be a tit-bit of gossip, if not scandal, tomorrow morning."

Anastasia looked at him apprehensively.

"What I am therefore going to suggest is that I stay here for some hours at least and lie on your bed."

He saw her expression and added quickly,

"You can trust me. I give you my word, Anastasia, I will not attempt to kiss you or touch you, although I would like to, until the invitation comes from you."

He smiled and asked,

"Is that reassuring?"

Anastasia was thinking quickly.

She realised that, if the King was thought not to have made love to her as his subjects would expect him to do and if in fact it was rumoured that he had slept in his own bedroom there would be only one explanation.

Everyone in Maurona would attribute it to the fact that his infatuation for the Comtesse le Graumont had blinded him to the attractions of his wife.

The King's suggestion was therefore extremely sensible.

"You are right! Whatever we do, we must not let anyone think or suggest that our marriage is not everything it should be."

"Very well," the King said. "I will do exactly what you want, Anastasia, and I shall hope that one day you will fall in love with me."

He smiled at her so beguilingly that for a moment she felt like saying,

'I think that I love you already! Please kiss me and I shall know if it is as exciting as I hope it will be.'

Then she saw the Comtesse's dark eyes looking up at him and remembered that they had spent the previous night together. She knew without being told that they would have 'made love'.

She felt a little shiver go through her.

The King might find her amusing. He might find her as attractive as he found the beautiful, extravagant ladies of Paris, but that was not what she wanted.

She wanted love, the love the Archbishop had spoken about in the marriage service, the idyllic love she had read about, the love that was a part of God.

"Thank you for being so kind and understanding," she said, and rose from the chair to stand looking at the King.

He was only about two feet away from her and she thought how easy it would be to move towards him, to feel his arms go round her. Then she could find out for herself whether she felt differently about him from the way she had felt about Christopher.

In her flat slippers she was very small and he seemed to tower above her.

"You are tired, Anastasia. You must go to sleep. Get into bed and I will lie here for a little while before I go back to my own room."

Anastasia moved towards the bed and while the King busied himself putting another log on the fire she drew off her blue wrap and threw it on a chair before slipping beneath the sheets.

He turned and saw her looking very small and insubstantial in the big bed with its huge golden canopy of carved angels chasing doves, surmounted by the Queen's crown.

"Shall I blow out the candles?" he asked.

"Yes, please," Anastasia replied.

The King blew out the candles on her side of the bed, and walking round, he extinguished those in the other candelabra.

He sat on the bed and then lay back against the pillows covering himself with the Venetian lace coverlet that was padded with eiderdown.

"Lie down and go to sleep, Anastasia," he said. "I am very comfortable, and I may in fact very easily fall asleep myself."

"What are we doing tomorrow?" she asked.

"If it pleases you, we could go driving in the morning. We can have luncheon at my Hunting Lodge which is some way outside the town, and then we can drive back at our leisure so that you can see the countryside."

"That sounds wonderful! I thought perhaps we would be going away on a honeymoon."

"As you have been travelling for so long," the King replied, "I thought you should have at least two days rest here. After that I have planned for us to go along the coast to a Villa I own near the French border. It has extensive gardens which are very beautiful at this time of the year."

"I would like that!" Anastasia said. She paused and added hesitatingly, "You do not – think you will be – bored being – alone with me?"

She wanted to add, "because we will not be making love!"

She was sure that was what brides and bridegrooms did on their honeymoon.

"If you continue to be as full of surprises as you have been up to date, I am quite sure, Anastasia, there is no question of my being bored!"

"I am glad about that," Anastasia said. "It is one thing that has frightened me more than anything else that you might find me dull."

"I think that possibility is too remote for me even to consider it. You are very unpredictable!"

Now there was no mistaking the mocking note in his deep voice.

There was silence.

Then after a long time Anastasia said in a slow sleepy voice,

"Are they very – beautiful?"

"Who?"

"The ladies – in Paris?"

The King thought before he answered,

"They are like pretty toys – gaily painted, brilliantly coloured."

He paused to add,

"They are made of granite, with a specially added magnetism which draws the coins from a man's pocket!"

Anastasia did not reply and he turned his head.

She was asleep!

In the light from the fire she appeared very young, very innocent and very vulnerable.

The King gazed at her for a long time.

Chapter Six

Anastasia awoke to find that she was alone.

For a moment it was difficult to remember what had happened the night before.

Then she recalled that she had talked to the King until gradually she found her voice getting slower and slower, and she must have fallen asleep even while they were still talking.

She turned her head now.

In the faint light of the sunshine coming into the room from the sides of the curtains, she could see the dent in the pillow where he had rested his head.

When he had left her, he must also have deliberately turned back the bedclothes to make it look as if he had been sleeping in the bed.

It had been a sensible idea, Anastasia thought, and would undoubtedly deceive the servants in the Palace. But she could not help wondering if anyone else had ever spent such a strange wedding night.

She had been relieved beyond words that the King had not been angry, as she had feared he would be when she had explained her feelings to him.

Now, lying in the great bed where many reigning Queens had slept before her, she wondered if they had been beset by a similar problem and if they too had been married knowing their husband cared for someone else.

An image of the Comtesse le Granmont came vividly to her mind. With her slanting, sensuous black eyes and her curving red mouth that seemed to suggest far more than she said in words, and the grace of her long neck and sinuous body Anastasia could see her attraction for men.

'She is so chic, so polished, so absolutely sure of herself,' Anastasia thought unhappily, and realised once again how young and ignorant she was.

But the King had been kind and understanding when she had told him she felt it would be wrong for them to make love together.

Hidden at the back of her mind had been the fear that he might overrule her arguments, not with words, but by insisting on his rights as her husband.

She had known that in that event there would be nothing she could do, no one to whom she could appeal for help. Yet she wondered now if it would have been as alarming or indeed as horrifying as she had told herself it would be.

But that was before she had seen him – that was when she had thought of him as stern, aloof, hard and inhuman.

In actual fact he was none of those things.

He was fascinating and attractive, and yet at the same time Anastasia admitted that she was still a little frightened of him.

She found herself wishing that she knew more about men and had more experience of them.

Then she thought she would know instinctively what she wanted, what she should do.

But what did she want?

The question seemed to leap out at her almost as if someone had spoken the words.

And she knew the answer.

She wanted to make the King fall in love with her.

She wanted him to love her, not the fascinating French Comtesse but her – his wife – and then, she knew irrefutably, she would love him.

When Olivia came to call her, drawing back the curtains to let in the golden sunshine, she began,

"I understand, Your Majesty, you will be driving this morning. It's a lovely day and you will find it warm in the sun. Nevertheless it would be wise for you to take a light jacket or a shawl with you."

"Am I to breakfast with His Majesty?" Anastasia asked.

She felt slightly embarrassed at asking the question, and wished she had consulted the King the night before as to what would be expected of her.

"You have slept late," Olivia replied, "and I think His Majesty has already breakfasted."

"In which case I would like my coffee here please, Olivia."

When Olivia had gone from the room, she rose from the bed and walked to the window to look out at the Palace gardens.

'What does the King feel this morning?' she asked herself. 'Is he looking forward to the day we will spend together or is he wishing he could be with the Comtesse le Granmont?'

There was, however, little time for such thoughts, for when Olivia returned it was to inform Anastasia that His Majesty had ordered the carriage to be round in an hour's time.

"I must not keep him waiting," Anastasia said quickly.

She descended the stairs five minutes before she thought he would be expecting her, but nevertheless one of the *aides-de-camp* still informed her that His Majesty was outside inspecting the horses.

As Anastasia walked down the steps, she saw a very elegant cabriolet of the latest design, which she was later to learn was the same model as those driven by all the smart gentlemen of Paris.

The King had purchased it on his last visit there, but it had taken some time for it to arrive in Maurona and this was to be the first time he would drive it.

Pulled by two superb black horses, it was painted in black and yellow and, Anastasia thought, it was a fitting complement to its driver, because the King himself was looking magnificent.

She had not seen him dressed in civilian clothes before, and she thought that he looked if anything more elegant out of uniform than when he was wearing it.

He swept his top hat from his head at her approach.

She had no idea how lovely she looked, wearing a pale yellow gown that she and Olivia had chosen with much care. It was deceptively simple because it had been very expensive, but the huge skirt accentuated the smallness of her waist and her bonnet was trimmed with satin kingcups, the colour relieved only by the green of their leaves.

"You look like a ray of sunshine!" the King remarked, as he raised her hand to his lips.

Flunkeys helped Anastasia into the cabriolet and the King took up the reins as the grooms sprang away from the horses' heads.

As they set off, Anastasia realised that behind them, keeping their distance, were two mounted soldiers.

The King saw her glance at them and explained,

"I am afraid we have to have an escort, but they will not interfere with us and will keep out of sight as much as possible. They know I dislike the feeling of being confined."

"It must be tiresome at times," Anastasia remarked.

As she spoke, she wondered if he realised that the servants knew that the Comtesse le Granmont came to the Palace to see him.

She could understand it would be impossible for him to go to her. How could the King ever move out of the Palace without being accompanied?

He turned his head to smile at her and she found herself forgetting everything but the joy of being beside him, knowing that they would have a whole day together without being surrounded by strangers.

Immediately after leaving the Palace the King had taken the road leading up into the woods that covered the side of the hills.

It twisted amongst the trees and after they had travelled some way, Anastasia could look back and see Sergei lying beneath them.

The white buildings, the trees bordering the streets and the vivid blue of the sea in the Bay were all were very lovely. But soon she could no longer see houses below, but only vineyards and acres of carnations.

Every so often the firs gave way to trees of mimosa, their golden bloom the same colour as Anastasia's gown.

As they drove on, the King described the countryside and she realised he knew a great deal about the agricultural difficulties and problems of his people, besides having an extensive knowledge of Mauronian history.

They drove on until the snow peaked mountains seemed a little nearer and the country became less densely inhabited.

Now the wild flowers were breathtaking.

Never had Anastasia imagined that wide expanses of ground could be a kaleidoscope of colour – pink, blue, yellow and white and the vivid scarlet poppies intermingled with the soft gentle pink of the wild orchids and the deep blue of the alpine gentians.

"It is all so beautiful!" she exclaimed. "I cannot understand why everyone does not wish to come to Maurona, if only for a holiday."

"I think that is something you and I should try to do in the future," the King said, "attract tourists to Sergei. It is far lovelier than Nice and yet crowds of people, including the English, flock there every winter. It is therefore exceedingly prosperous."

Without thinking Anastasia replied,

"Perhaps that is why the Emperor would wish to annex it for France."

"That is untrue," the King replied sharply. "Who has been telling you such lies? The Emperor assured me himself that he has no designs on Nice, and I believe him, just as I believe that he is not concerned with Maurona."

Anastasia wanted to argue that that might be his opinion, but a great many people thought otherwise.

Then she told herself she had no substantial facts with which to backup such an argument.

As she did not speak, the King went on,

"I know quite well what your Foreign Secretary, Lord John Russell, thinks. I have heard the same forebodings from the Spanish. But the Emperor is my friend and I trust him! So I can assure you categorically, Anastasia, these lies are perpetrated about him only because other Nations are jealous."

"I am sure you are right," Anastasia said. "At the same time, the reason why Queen Victoria wished me to marry you was to help maintain the independence of Maurona."

"That is undoubtedly what you have done," the King said firmly, "so we need have no further heart-searching where the French are concerned."

He paused to add in a more gentle tone,

"One day I will take you to Paris. You shall meet my friend the Emperor and his very beautiful wife, the Empress Eugenie. You will then be convinced how quite unnecessary your fears are."

"Forgive me for – mentioning it," Anastasia said.

"There is nothing to forgive. We must always speak frankly with each other, Anastasia, just as you spoke frankly to me last night. Nothing could be more disastrous than for us to have reservations or secrets from each other."

Anastasia thought guiltily that already she had secrets from him, in that she was intriguing with Olivia and had taken the advice of Captain Aznar.

Then she told herself that those secrets did not count. They were only because she was trying to do her best, not only for Maurona, but also for the King himself.

And there was no doubt that he had his personal secrets where the Comtesse was concerned.

Even to think of the fascinating Frenchwoman was to feel that a shadow of darkness dimmed the brilliance of the sunshine.

Then, resolutely, Anastasia forced herself to forget everything in an effort to amuse the King.

She told him about her Christmas at Windsor and made him laugh at her description of the cold of the Castle, the stiffness of the courtiers and the disapproval of the Queen when the revellers were noisy at their card games.

"It sounds exactly like what I had to endure when my father was alive," the King said.

"Was it very formal?"

"Intolerably so! One could hardly breathe without permission and every form of personal expression was frowned upon."

She knew by the tone of his voice how much he had disliked it and she said eagerly,

"Do not let us have a Court like that. Let us encourage people with talents to feel they are welcome at the Palace. I would like to meet writers, artists and musicians. I would really prefer always to be surrounded by brains rather than by blue blood."

"I think you are too clever already!" the King remarked.

"Too clever?"

"You frighten me," he replied, "and a beautiful woman is not required to have brains."

"That contention is completely out of date, as you well know," Anastasia rejoined. "If the newspapers are to be believed, there are women all over the world who are beginning to speak their minds."

"And who do you think is going to listen to them?" the King teased.

"One day you will have to do so. I know at the moment we have no rights, we are only the chattels of our husbands. But I feel sure the day will come when women will have more power and more consequence than they have now."

"God help us poor men!" the King said with an exaggerated groan.

Then he asked more seriously,

"Why are you not content just to be as you look? A pretty flower created by God for the delight of man!"

"Because pretty flowers die!" Anastasia retorted. "I want to live and I want to live fully!"

The King took his eyes from his horses to look at her.

"That is something I feel quite certain you will do, sooner or later!" he answered. "But I am not certain yet if it will be very satisfactory from my point of view."

Anastasia did not quite understand what he was saying and to change the subject, pointed out a castle in the distance and asked the King to tell her about it.

They reached the Hunting Lodge, which was a small house situated in the depths of a pine forest and found that luncheon was waiting for them.

They were waited upon by servants, all clothed in national dress, who looked after the Lodge. The food was good, if plain, and the wines came from an adjacent vineyard.

Seated in the small dining room with a table undecorated except for a bowl of flowers, Anastasia thought it was delightful for them to have a meal alone, while there was nothing about her companion to remind her that he was a reigning monarch.

"What are you thinking?" the King asked when she had been silent for a few moments.

"I was thinking," she replied, "how much easier it is to talk to you like this. You are not so awe-inspiring here as you are when in the Palace."

"What you are saying," he replied in his deep voice, "is that now you are thinking of me as a man."

"Yes, that is just what I was trying to say," Anastasia replied.

She smiled as she spoke.

Then her eyes met his, and for a moment it was impossible to move.

She found herself held in a way she could not explain. It was almost as if he was drawing her towards him and it was hard to resist.

He had not moved, and yet she felt as if he had put out his arms round her. For a moment Anastasia found it difficult to breathe.

She did not know what she felt. It was a strange sensation she had never experienced before and, because she was shy, her eyes dropped before his.

"Last night, Anastasia, you challenged me."

Anastasia raised her eyes in surprise.

"It is a challenge I have accepted," the King went on, "to make you love me."

The colour rose in Anastasia's cheeks.

"I do not – think – " she murmured, "that I meant – it – like that."

"What you said," the King continued, his eyes on her face, "was that the man you will love must captivate your mind – and that is what I intend to do."

Anastasia felt her heart give a leap, almost as if it turned over in her breast. It was a feeling half pleasure, half pain.

"Always in the past, I have desired and made love to a woman's body. It is a new experience for me to learn that I must woo your mind – that intelligent, unpredictable little mind which both intrigues and surprises me."

There was a note in his voice that made Anastasia feel as if she vibrated to music.

The King was watching her and after a moment he said very softly,

"But may I be allowed to say that you are also very lovely and very – desirable?"

Once again Anastasia found it impossible to look at him. There was an expression in his eyes, which made her quiver. It seemed to her there was a fire in the darkness of them, but she could not be sure.

"Are you capable of love, Anastasia?" the King asked her.

He waited, and as if he compelled her to answer, she replied after a moment,

"Why should you – think I might – not be?"

"Because," he replied, "many English women are cold and restrained and what they would mean by the word *'love'* is not what I mean by love."

"What does it mean to you?" Anastasia asked as if she could not help herself.

"I am from the sun," the King replied, "and to me love is an unquenchable fire, burning through every nerve and sinew of the body until one is utterly and completely consumed by the wonder of it."

His voice made Anastasia feel as if he had blown a fanfare of trumpets.

"Would you stand aside from such a conflagration, Anastasia?" he asked, "or could you surrender yourself wholly to the fire of love?"

There was silence and then hesitatingly Anastasia answered,

"Mama said that a lady always – conducts herself with – reserve and self-control – her husband would not *'expect otherwise'.*"

"That is your mother's point of view," the King said softly, "and it is what I would expect her to think. But you, Anastasia, are different. Is that how you expect and want to behave when you fall in love?"

As he spoke, Anastasia knew that her mother's attitude was not what she had dreamt and hoped to find some day. It was a touch of fire she had expected to feel when Christopher touched her, but it had not been there. It was a flicker of fire she felt deep inside when she thought of a man's lips on hers.

Her face was very expressive and after a moment the King said,

"I am waiting for an answer."

There was a pause, and then Anastasia replied hesitatingly,

"I – want to be *really* in – love – and I know it will be – very exciting – and very wonderful."

She paused and added almost in a whisper,

"Like flying into the sky to touch the stars or diving deep down to the very bottom of the sea!"

Her eyes met the King's and Anastasia felt herself tremble.

"That is what you shall feel," he murmured quietly.

There was a silence which seemed to be full of an inexplicable magic.

Then abruptly the King rose from the table.

"I think we should go back," he said in a very different tone. "We have driven here through the mountains and I want to take you home by the valleys. It is a longer route, but you will see the villages and the people over whom you now rule."

"I would like that."

She felt so emotionally moved that it was difficult to speak naturally.

She too rose from the table and walked to the window to look out at the amazing view over the countryside.

Far away in the distance she could just see a glimmer of blue sea. Nearer there was soft undulating land, much of it green with vines, the rest vivid with flowers.

She stood looking out and then became aware that the King had drawn nearer until he was standing just behind her.

She had taken off her bonnet before luncheon and the sunshine was golden on her fair hair and her eyes looked very blue, as she turned round involuntarily to say to him,

"It is yours! Your world!"

His eyes were on her face as he replied,

"Yet you told me yesterday that I had to conquer it, or be conquered."

"It is difficult to put into words, but perhaps the easiest way to conquer a country is through the hearts of its people."

The King's lips twisted a little cynically.

"I often wonder," he said, "how the hearts of the people would react if it came to the crunch. Would their affection stand the strain? Would they fight for their so-called loyalty to the Crown?"

Anastasia thought before she answered him,

"I think that one has to win their trust and faith. People, ordinary people, need to believe in those who rule them, and they must also be convinced that their rulers

~ 164 ~

are right – right in their judgements and right in their actions."

"Who taught you these things?" the King asked sharply.

Anastasia looked at him in surprise.

"No one!" she answered. "I am just saying what I think and perhaps it is foolish! But I have never had a chance to discuss my ideas with anyone before."

"Is that the truth, Anastasia?"

"Why should I tell you anything but the truth?"

"Because you sound as if you have been sitting at the feet of Statesmen and they have put into your mind all the ideas they think I ought to hear."

Anastasia laughed.

"I wish I could make you understand that until I became of consequence by becoming your future bride, no Statesman had ever condescended to talk to anyone so insignificant."

She smiled as she added,

"Lord John Russell spent half an hour at Hampton Court Palace after I had been told I was to come to Maurona and the Prime Minister, Lord Palmerston, paid me some very pretty compliments at number 10 Downing Street. Otherwise, I promise you, my life has been very dull and quiet and Mama has spent her time telling me I do not behave with enough circumspection."

The King laughed.

"You paint a very sad picture, Anastasia! If it is true, the butterfly has certainly shed its cocoon and is now a very dazzling creature!"

"First I am a flower – now I am a butterfly!" Anastasia said pretending to be affronted, "and I do so want someone to take me seriously."

The King laughed again.

"I promise you that they will put up a statue to you when you die. It will be on the Marine Parade and every man shall take off his hat to you as he passes!"

"While the seagulls and the pigeons will treat it most disrespectfully!" Anastasia flashed.

The King was still laughing,

"Come along, I am taking you home. I think you have lectured me enough for one day."

"I did not mean to do so," Anastasia said quickly, "please believe me! I was only putting my own thoughts into words."

"That is what frightens me," the King remarked.

She could not quite make up her mind if he was annoyed by what she had said to him or whether he was, despite himself, rather impressed,

There was so much to see on their way home that it was difficult to have much serious conversation, but Anastasia was acutely conscious of the man beside her – a man who was wooing her mind.

When they arrived back at the Palace, there were various matters for the King to attend to and Anastasia went up to her own suite.

She found the boudoir opening off her bedroom filled with bouquets and flowers, which had been sent to her by some of the people she had met the previous day.

There was also, Olivia told her, in another room a great pile of wedding presents that had arrived to swell those at which Anastasia had only glanced briefly the morning before the wedding.

'I will look at them tomorrow,' she told herself and went into her bedroom to take off her yellow gown.

She lay down for a little while, then had her bath and was ready to join the King in the private dining room in the King's Suite.

There were innumerable rooms set aside for the private apartments of the King and Queen. Each had a sitting room, a private dining room and a small reception room where they could entertain rather than in the large Staterooms downstairs.

There were rooms for the Ladies-in-Waiting and the *aides-de-camp*, and a secretarial office.

The King's dining room was furnished in the French style and there were some extremely fine pictures on the walls, besides Louis XIV gilt side tables that Anastasia learnt had come from the Palace at Versailles.

She wondered if the Emperor of the French had ever wanted to take them back and then told herself that would be an indiscreet question to ask.

It might also put generous ideas into the King's head, so she contented herself with admiring the dining room table which, unlike the one on which they had eaten their luncheon, was decorated with gold ornaments and exotic orchids.

"I said we would dispense with as much formality as possible while we were on our honeymoon," the King explained as they sat down. "I knew it was what you would prefer, Anastasia, until you become used to the intolerable Court custom of having someone always breathing down your neck."

"I have enjoyed today," Anastasia admitted softly.

"So have I," he answered and for no real reason she found herself blushing.

The chef had obviously wanted to excel himself on the first night of their honeymoon, and long before the dinner had come to an end, Anastasia declared with a little sigh that she could eat no more.

"You have such delicious food," she sighed, "I shall become as fat as a German *Frau* and none of my beautiful new gowns will fit me."

"I never think of you as having German blood," the King said, and remembered he had said very much the same thing once before.

"I find it hard to think of it too, but Papa was half English and his grandmother was Austrian. So I think the truth is that I am rather a mongrel, if predominantly English."

"Now I understand!" the King exclaimed with a twinkle in his eye. "Mongrels are believed to be far more intelligent than pedigree dogs."

"You are making me nervous," Anastasia said. "I shall definitely have to think before I speak, as Mama has always begged me to do and in consequence I shall only make the most inane and nonsensical remarks."

"I like you just as you are, Anastasia"

Once again their eyes met and the expression in his made her feel shy and strange in an exciting way.

They sat talking for a long time at the table.

The King told Anastasia many historical facts about the Mediterranean countries she had not known before.

"The Greeks worshipped Aphrodite as the Goddess of Love," he said, "and the Romans called her Venus."

He paused then asked,

"If you had the choice, Anastasia, would you like to be the Goddess of Love or the Goddess of Learning?"

Anastasia thought in some way he was testing her, but she answered honestly and quite seriously,

"I would – rather be the Goddess of Love."

Seeing a sudden glint in the King's eyes she knew it was the reply he wanted and she could not prevent the colour rising in her cheeks.

She rose from the table and they went next door into the sitting room.

It was very comfortable and more masculine than any other room Anastasia had seen in the Palace.

There were deep leather armchairs, sporting prints on the walls and a number of trophies that the King had shot at one time or another. There were the heads of a wild boar and a bear, several antlers, some stags' horns and some lesser but rarer deer, all labelled with the year in which they had been shot.

Anastasia was just asking him to tell her some of his sporting experiences when a servant came into the room with a note on a gold salver.

"This has been brought for Your Majesty," he announced as he bowed, "and it is of the utmost urgency!"

Anastasia glanced at the envelope as the King picked it up. She could see the insignia on the back and was certain it incorporated the fleur-de-lis.

"Please forgive me, Anastasia," he, said as the flunkey handed him a pointed letter opener.

He slit the top of the envelope and drew out a piece of writing paper.

Anastasia longed to know what it contained. It could not have been a long letter, for the King barely glanced at it before he said,

"Inform the messenger that the request is granted."

The flunkey bowed and went from the room.

There was a silence during which Anastasia was certain that the King was choosing his words with care.

After a moment he said,

"There is someone I have to see. It will not take long. It is, I understand, a matter of importance."

"But of course. Shall I wait here for you?"

The King glanced at the clock.

"I feel you must still be tired after the exhaustion of yesterday. Why do you not go to bed, Anastasia? I will come to you later."

"Yes, of course," Anastasia replied, "but please don't be too long or I shall fall asleep. I have a lot more subjects I wish to discuss with you."

She smiled as she spoke but the King was not looking at her.

He turned and opened not the door onto the corridor as she had expected, but that into the dining room they had just left.

Anastasia had already realised that in the King's apartments, as in her own, all the rooms were intercommunicating so that she could move from one to the other without encountering the sentries who were stationed outside in the corridors.

The King closed the door of the sitting room behind him and with a little throb of her heart she was quite certain that he was going to the farthest end of his suite, to his private room where there was a staircase to the ground floor.

'And who would be meeting him there but the Comtesse?' she asked herself.

She could not be certain, but somehow her suspicions seemed very compelling. She felt a sudden blaze of anger that the end of their happy day together, the first day of their honeymoon, had been disrupted by the Frenchwoman and her note.

Anastasia pulled open the door leading from the sitting room into the King's bedroom.

She had no intention of returning to her own suite by means of the corridor, when she would be seen by the sentries, who would then be aware that the King had left her alone.

She passed through his bedroom without noticing the magnificence of it and went through the communicating door into her own room.

The fire was burning in the grate and the candelabra were lit on the dressing table and beside the bed.

There was the fragrance of flowers and the whole room seemed welcoming and very attractive, but

Anastasia was deep in her own thoughts as she moved towards the bell pull.

Before she reached it, the door opened and Olivia came in.

"Your – Majesty!" she started in a strangled voice and Anastasia turned round.

"What is it?" she asked.

"Pedro has just – told me that a revolution is to – *break out tonight*!" Olivia gasped.

"What do you mean?" Anastasia enquired.

"*It is a plot*! A plot – Your Majesty – and you must – save the King!"

"But how – what has happened? Speak slowly, Olivia,"

She realised Olivia must have been running through the long corridors of the Palace to reach her.

"Pedro overheard – everything. The Ambassador was – instructing the men who are to – kidnap His Majesty."

"*Kidnap him?*" Anastasia exclaimed. "Where? How?"

"It is all arranged, Your Majesty. The Comtesse le Granmont will be with him for a short while and then when he sees her off through the door into the garden he will be seized. A carriage will be waiting outside the Palace wall to carry His Majesty over the French border."

Olivia paused for breath and Anastasia cried,

"Go on!"

"Once he is on French soil, the revolution will break out and His Majesty will ask the French – or be forced to do so – to intervene. They will march into Sergei at his request and once here the country will be theirs!"

Anastasia's eyes were very large in her small face as she stared at Olivia and her brain assimilated all she had been told.

It was a very clever plot!

If the French put down the revolution at the King's invitation, Queen Victoria, indeed the world, could not charge them with aggression!

The only thing that could save Maurona was for the King not to be kidnapped.

Olivia was staring at her white-faced.

"Fetch Captain Aznar!" Anastasia commanded. "Fetch him quickly!"

Olivia ran from the room as Anastasia stood trying to think what to do.

It seemed to Anastasia that she waited for a very long time before the door opened again and Olivia reappeared with Captain Aznar. In reality it was only a few minutes, for the Captain had been in the *aides-de-camp's* room of the on the ground floor.

"Captain Aznar, Your Majesty!" Olivia called out, her voice still breathless.

Anastasia waited until the door was closed then she cried,

"Olivia has brought me terrible news! Tell the Captain, Olivia, what you have just told me."

A little less breathlessly, but still a trifle incoherently Olivia gasped out her story.

"Pedro is to be relied upon," Anastasia said as she finished. "He is First Valet to the French Ambassador."

Captain Aznar looked at Anastasia.

"We must get His Majesty away."

"Where to?" Anastasia asked.

"To the Army in Leziga," Captain Aznar replied.

"You will take me with you?"

"Of course, ma'am! We would not leave you to the revolutionaries."

"We will need horses."

"I will arrange that," Captain Aznar replied, "and there are three Officers in the Palace at the moment who can be trusted."

"Will you arrange everything, Captain?"

"At once," Captain Aznar replied, "but we must alert His Majesty. Is he in his rooms?"

Anastasia hesitated.

She could not bear to tell him where she suspected the King would be at this moment.

"I will tell His Majesty," she said firmly.

"I need not remind you that there is no time to be lost, ma'am. If they fail to kidnap the King from the Palace, the revolutionaries in their pay might find another way to take him prisoner."

"We will be ready as soon as you have the horses."

Captain Aznar bowed.

Then, as he turned quickly to leave the room, Anastasia called out,

"One moment! Has the King an old nanny who is living, or someone he knew well as a child?"

"His Majesty's old nanny," Captain Aznar replied, "is alive, but she was too old to come to the wedding. She lives a long way from Serge, in a village in the Pyrenees."

"Thank you, Captain. That is all I wanted to know,"

She opened the communicating door as she spoke and, without looking back, started to run through the King's apartments. She moved from one to the other until finally, beyond the reception room, she came to a door which she knew led into the King's private room.

Just for a moment she hesitated.

Then, drawing a deep breath and putting up her chin in an instinctive effort to be brave, she opened the door and walked in.

The room was dimly lit and smaller than Anastasia had expected.

Seated on a huge divan heaped with satin cushions was the Comtesse le Granmont – and standing in front of her was the King.

Anastasia had the impression that they were arguing with each other, but at her appearance their voices died away and their faces were turned towards her with an almost ludicrous expression of surprise on them.

"Please forgive me for interrupting you," Anastasia began, to the King, "but I have in my sitting room a dear old woman who was your nanny. She came to the wedding yesterday and has tried ineffectually to see you all today before she returns home."

She paused to say softly,

"I feel she will not live very long and it would make her so very happy if she could see you – perhaps for the last time."

For a moment it seemed as if the King could not find his voice and then he answered,

"Yes, of course, I will speak to her."

With a charming smile Anastasia turned towards the Comtesse who had not risen and was still seated on the divan,

"I do apologise for interrupting you, *madame*," she said, "but through a whole series of misunderstandings the King was not informed earlier today that his old nanny had called."

Very reluctantly and with stormy eyes, the Comtesse rose to her feet.

Looking at her, Anastasia thought it impossible for any lady of good breeding to wear a dress that was so improper and so revealing.

Yet she had to admit that the Comtesse looked extremely alluring and the rubies round her neck and in her ears must have cost someone a small fortune.

Anastasia wondered if they had been a present from the King, but hastily reminded herself there was no time to be lost in speculations of that sort.

"I will not keep you more than five or ten minutes," she turned to the King, "and you will make someone who loves you very happy."

For the first time since Anastasia had entered the room, the King glanced towards the Comtesse.

It was as if, without words, he asked her to leave.

"I will wait for you, Sire," she stated firmly.

As if he felt it was hopeless to argue, the King merely followed Anastasia through the door.

She waited until he had closed it behind them, then she slipped her hand into his.

"Come quickly!" she whispered.

She started to pull him across the reception room.

"What is this and why the urgency, Anastasia?" he enquired.

"I will tell you when we reach your bedroom."

She could not help feeling afraid that the Comtesse might hear them or there might perhaps be other ears lurking in the shadows or behind the curtains covering the windows.

When things such as the plot that threatened the King happened, who could one trust?

While she was pulling him forward, the King walked quickly and then as they reached his bedroom he said in an irritated tone,

"What is this all about? Is my old nanny really here?"

"No! That was merely an excuse so that I could tell you what has been planned," Anastasia cried. "The French mean to kidnap you when you take the Comtesse downstairs. They will take you through the door in the Palace wall to where a carriage is waiting to carry you across the border."

She saw by the King's expression that he did not believe her.

"Everything is planned," she went on hurriedly. "As soon as you have been abducted, a revolution will break out in the City, and because you have no alternative you will have to ask the French to help you to restore order."

"Who told you all this nonsense?" the King asked sharply.

"It is the truth," Anastasia insisted. "I swear to you it is the truth!"

"Do you really believe I would invite the French to march into Sergei?" the King asked.

"Once you are with your so-called '*friends*'," Anastasia retorted, "do you imagine you would get a truthful report of what is happening? What would you do if you were told that the whole City was being devastated, women and children being killed, the Palace looted? Under such circumstances what other alternative would there be but to ask for their help?"

"I cannot believe there is such a plot!" the King exclaimed angrily. "But if there is, what do you suggest I do?"

"Several of your Officers here in the Palace, who are to be trusted, will help you to reach the Army. If a revolution breaks out, it can be dealt with by you – not by a foreign power!"

He stared at her as if she had taken leave of her senses.

Then, as they looked at each other in silence, the door opened and Captain Aznar came in.

The King turned to him.

"Are you a part of these ridiculous theatricals, Aznar?" he enquired hastily. "Can I possibly credit that what the Queen has told me is the truth?"

"You can believe it, Sire," Captain Aznar replied quietly. "It is indeed what some of us have been expecting for a long time."

The King looked at him in astonishment.

"You really thought this might happen?"

"This, or something like it, Sire," Captain Aznar answered. "It is only Her Majesty who has been clever enough to discover the details of the plot, before it is put into operation."

The King looked back at Anastasia and seemed to hesitate.

Then Captain Aznar added,

"I am certain, Sire, that the coast road will be blocked and so will both passes. To reach Leziga we shall have to ride over the mountains."

"I cannot believe it! This is quite incredible!" the King exclaimed.

"It would be folly, Sire, for you to risk the chance that I am wrong! I therefore suggest that we leave as quickly as possible. Will you change your clothes?"

"And I must change mine!" Anastasia said.

"Please be as swift as possible, ma'am," Captain Aznar begged.

Without saying anything more, Anastasia ran into her own room.

Olivia was waiting for her and already had laid out one of the new riding habits, which she had brought with her from England.

It took her only a few minutes to take off her evening gown and put on the riding habit of sapphire blue velvet, frogged with white braid.

There was a very elegant tall hat to go with it, but Anastasia covered her head with a white chiffon scarf, wrapping the long ends round her neck.

"The King is going to Leziga, Olivia," she said when she was ready. "I shall be with him. Join me as soon as you can."

"I will do that, Your Majesty."

"And I should not allow your Pedro to go back to the French Embassy," Anastasia went on. "It might be dangerous for him."

"He has already thought of that, Your Majesty."

Anastasia looked at her.

"Thank you, with all my heart," she murmured softly.

Then she bent forward to kiss Olivia on the cheek.

She glanced at the clock. It was now twenty minutes past eleven.

She had a feeling that the plotters would start the revolution in the early hours of the morning. By that time they would expect their plans to have materialised and the King would be over the French border.

It would have taken some time before the Palace guards were alerted to the riots taking place in the centre of the City.

She entered the King's bedroom and found he had changed into uniform.

Captain Aznar was still with him.

"I have a Cavalry cloak here for you, ma'am, ," he said to Anastasia. "You will find it a warm and effective disguise. His Majesty will also be wearing one."

"Thank you, Captain."

He put it over her shoulders. Of heavy black wool, the cloak had a hood designed to cover an Officer's cap.

Pulled over Anastasia's head it hid her face almost completely and, because she was so small, it reached almost to the ground.

The King swung a similar cloak over his shoulders.

Then without speaking they followed Captain Aznar across the corridor and down the secondary staircase, which brought them to the ground floor.

Here they hurried along dark passages in a part of the Palace Anastasia guessed was used as offices, or occupied by the servants.

After they had walked for a long way, they came to a door that Captain Aznar opened.

Outside three men similarly cloaked were waiting, already on horseback, each holding a second horse by the bridle. It was difficult for the King to identify them in the darkness.

"Captain Seiza, Captain Mauresa and Lieutenant Tuleda, Sire," Captain Aznar said in a low voice.

The Officers saluted and the King swung himself into the saddle of a large black stallion, while Captain Aznar assisted Anastasia onto a horse, which she was thankful to see, was carrying a side-saddle.

Two of the Officers went ahead, the King and Anastasia followed them and Captain Aznar and Lieutenant Tuleda brought up the rear.

They were riding, Anastasia realised, at the back of the Palace. First she saw sheds and outbuildings, and then they were on a narrow drive leading to what was obviously a side gate, perhaps one used by tradesmen.

There were two sentries guarding it who came to attention when they saw the Officers.

The gates were opened and they passed through them without hurry.

Only when they were outside and a little way from the Palace did the leading Officers quicken their pace.

As soon as they were free of the barracks and various other buildings outside the Palace wall they moved even quicker. Soon they were riding among the forest trees as Anastasia and the King had done earlier in the day.

It was a brilliant starlit night and a half moon was creeping up the sky, giving them just enough light to be able to see where they were going.

After travelling a short distance they left the narrow road and took to the mountainside. Here there were only tracks and they proceeded in single file.

No one spoke and there was only the sound of jingling bridles, the horses' hoofs and the occasional dry cough from one of the animals.

On and on they climbed, rising higher and always higher.

They had ridden for very nearly an hour when the King pulled his horse to a standstill on a small flat plateau.

He turned to look back.

Moving up beside him Anastasia did the same.

Below them lay Sergei. Most of the houses were in darkness, but in the very centre of the town there was the brilliant light of a fire.

The flames were vividly red against the darkness and then, as they watched, another fire burst into flame a little to the right of it and then there was another to the left.

"The revolution has already started, Sire!" Captain Aznar muttered.

Without replying, the King turned his horse and once again they were climbing.

Up, up, up!

The cold from the snows was now sharp against Anastasia's face and her small nose began to feel as if it did not belong to her.

Still they went on and now the horses were wheezing and sweating a little with the effort, until finally when Anastasia was sure that they must be nearly at the top of the mountain, the Officers in front of them came to a standstill.

Captain Aznar passed Anastasia to reach the King's side.

"These are the old caves, Sire. You may remember that at one time certain mining operations took place here. I think this is where we should rest."

The King turned his head, but he did not speak.

"It would be dangerous to descend on the other side of the mountain, which is very steep, until we can clearly see the way," Captain Aznar said. "What I suggest, Sire, is that we wait here until dawn and then proceed to Leziga."

"Very well," the King agreed.

He dismounted as he spoke and went to Anastasia's side to lift her down from the saddle.

As she felt his arms around her, she longed to hold on to him.

It had been frightening to see the fires down below them in Sergei. It was even more frightening to think this was a deliberate attempt to deprive the King of his country or to make him merely a puppet under the jurisdiction of the French.

The Officers were taking things from their saddlebags.

Now one man had gone ahead of them into the caves and a moment later they saw a faint light.

"Will you go in, Sire?" Captain Aznar asked. "We don't wish to draw attention to ourselves. A light on the mountain might be suspicious."

"Of course."

The King put his arm round Anastasia and drew her forward over the rough ground.

She expected the entrance to the cave to be low, but the King did not have to bend his head and she found herself walking down what appeared to be a rough stone passage to where a light was gleaming at the end of it.

This led to a large cave, but the Officer holding the candle lantern went further still until they entered another cave not as big as the first one, but nevertheless quite an appreciable size.

He held up the lantern and Anastasia could see there was a pile of straw on the ground in one corner, a wooden packing case in the centre and several large logs of wood to sit on.

"This appears to have been in use," the King remarked.

"In the winter it is a shelter, Sire, for mountaineers or shepherds who become snowbound," the Officer answered. "I used to come here as a boy!"

"I believe I have been here once before," the King reflected.

The Officer put the lantern on a packing case.

"I will see if I can find anything to make you more comfortable, ma'am," he said to Anastasia.

He went back to the other cave and by the sounds coming from it Anastasia guessed that the Officers had brought their horses into it with them.

A moment later Captain Aznar appeared. He had a flask in his hand.

"I thought, Sire, you might like something to keep out the cold," he suggested. "Regrettably, I forgot to bring a glass."

"I dare say we shall manage, Captain."

Captain Aznar handed the King the flask and Anastasia saw that under his other arm he carried a blanket.

He spread it over the straw.

"At least it will keep you clean, ma'am," he said. "I am afraid that in the hurry to get away we did not think to bring more than one blanket between us."

"I am sure we will be quite comfortable," Anastasia smiled.

"If there is anything you want, Sire," Captain Aznar said to the King, "you know we will try to provide it."

He bowed.

"Thank you, Aznar. There is no need for me to tell you how grateful I am."

"No need at all, Your Majesty."

He disappeared and Anastasia looked a little apprehensively at the King.

She was not certain of his feelings. She had known he had been angry, very angry, when she had told him what his *'friends'* had planned.

She had thought when they rode away from the Palace that he still did not believe her, and she kept wondering what would happen if Olivia had been mistaken. Suppose there was no revolution and the whole plot had been something dreamed up by Pedro?

Then, when she saw the fires in the City, she had known there had been no mistake. The revolution had begun and she and Captain Aznar had saved the King from humiliation and defeat.

The King held out the flask.

"Drink a little," he suggested. "It will keep you from catching cold."

As she was anxious to please him, she obeyed, even while she disliked the taste of the fiery brandy, which seemed to sear its way through her body.

"A little more," the King ordered and she took another sip rather than argue.

He drank from the flask and then set it down beside the lantern on the packing case.

"You had better lie down, Anastasia," he said.

She pushed back the hood from her head and then unfastened the clasp at her neck.

Vaguely she thought she would cover herself with it when she lay down on the blanket.

The King sat down on one of the logs with his back to her.

For a moment he seemed to be staring into space. Then, as she stood irresolute, looking at him, he said in a low voice,

"You were right! I have made a ghastly mess of – everything."

There was so much pain in his voice that instinctively Anastasia moved towards him. Then without thinking, impulsively she put an arm round his shoulders.

"It will be all right," she said soothingly. "I am sure it will be all right!"

He turned towards her and quite naturally, like a child who wants to be comforted, be turned his face against her breast.

"How could I have been such a fool?" he asked and the self-accusation in his tone was even more poignant than the pain she had heard before.

"You will win!" she told him confidently, "I know you will!"

He did not answer and she felt his head heavy against her. Now with both her arms enfolding him, she thought that he was more like her son than her husband.

She wanted to comfort him, she wanted to help him and she wanted above all to give him courage.

But, because it was difficult to find the words, she could only hold him close against her and pray with all her heart that everything would be all right.

Chapter Seven

The King did not speak and after a little while Anastasia said gently,

"I think you should rest. There will be much for you to do tomorrow."

As she spoke, she shivered with the cold and the King raised his head.

"You have taken off your cloak," he said almost accusingly. "Lie down, Anastasia, and I will cover you with it."

"You must – lie down – too."

For a moment she thought he was going to refuse her.

Then, as she lay down on the blanket that covered the straw, he bent over to cover her with the heavy, wide Cavalry cloak, before he lowered himself to lie beside her and spread over them both his own cloak as if it was another blanket.

For a moment they lay side by side, the light from the candle lantern flickering in the breeze and casting strange shadows on the arched ceiling of the cave.

"It is going to get still colder as the night goes on," the King reflected after a moment. "May I suggest, Anastasia, that you come nearer to me? The only way to avoid the chill from the snows will be for us to keep close to each other."

As if he sensed her hesitation, he added,

"I am quite sure that the Officers in the outer cavern are lying against their horses. It is something we are taught to do on manoeuvres. Nights in the mountains can be bitterly cold."

Feeling a trifle self-conscious, Anastasia moved towards him.

He put his arm round her and she laid her head against his shoulder, but as she did so she gave a little cry.

"What is it?" he asked.

"I hurt my cheek on one of your decorations."

"I will take them off and throw them away," he said. "I have no right to them."

He spoke so violently that Anastasia cried,

"No – you must not think like that! They are, I am sure, mostly Mauronian – and you can be proud of them."

The King did not answer and after a moment she added,

"Whatever happens you must not be humble."

"Why not?" he asked harshly. "I can assure you I feel not only humble, but humiliated."

"You made a mistake. Your people will understand that, but they will want you to be strong and resolute. They must have someone to follow, someone they can believe in."

The King did not reply and after a pause she commented,

"A strong man can have a limb amputated because it is gangrenous and he will survive, but a weak man will die – even though the rest of his body is unaffected."

"I trusted the Emperor," the King said as if he spoke to himself.

"And now you have found that he is untrustworthy. I can well understand it is very hurtful when someone whom we trust proves unworthy of our faith. But there is one thing that really matters now, that you should rid the country of the traitors and restore the pride that I am sure every Mauronian feels in his own land."

"Do you believe I can do it?" the King asked.

"I know you can," Anastasia said positively. "As I said to you on the first day we met – you are exactly what a King should be. That is the – Sovereign your people will want to follow."

She felt the King draw in his breath.

Then she laid her face a little gingerly against his shoulder so that the decorations would not hurt her and felt his arm tighten around her.

"Do you believe in me, Anastasia? Honestly and sincerely and with your whole heart?"

"I believe in you," she said with a solemnity that seemed to make the words sound like a vow.

The King was silent and then he mumbled,

"Thank you. Thank you, Anastasia."

There was silence again.

Then, because even with the heavy cloak covering her, Anastasia still felt cold she instinctively moved a little closer.

As she did so, she felt a sensation she had never known before. It was strange yet exciting, a little frightening yet wonderful.

Almost without meaning to – obeying the impulse of her body rather than her will – she drew nearer still.

Now her whole body was touching his.

She felt he was deep in introspection and because she did not wish him to be too depressed she said with a deliberate note of amusement in her voice,

"We are certainly reversing the usual procedure in romances. This is not 'rags to riches', but from 'Palace to a bundle of straw!'"

"And certainly a very strange honeymoon." the King added.

"When we are old, it will be an adventure that we can recount to our grandchildren."

"How many are you envisaging we might have?"

"Perhaps a dozen or so," Anastasia said lightly. "Who knows?"

"That is, of course, a question for you to answer. One cannot have grandchildren without first having children and one cannot have children without first making love, Anastasia."

He felt that she was suddenly tense and he added reassuringly,

"However, we have other things to talk about at the moment. But before you go to sleep, I must try to thank you."

"Wait until it is all over," Anastasia begged. "Perhaps it was a mistake to come away. Perhaps you should have met the rioters on the steps of the Palace and – defied them."

"That would have meant unnecessary bloodshed," the King replied, "and Maurona would have been left without a Ruler."

"At least you are – safe."

"Exactly what that means we shall know tomorrow."

Anastasia would have said more, but before she could speak the King suggested,

"Try to rest. You have had a long day following an exhausting wedding and an even more tiring journey. You could not have foreseen that anything like this would happen when you left the quietness and security of England."

"Whatever happens tomorrow," Anastasia whispered, "I shall always be glad – very, very glad – that I came."

*

She must have slept, and yet it seemed to her she had only just closed her eyes when Captain Aznar's voice startled her into wakefulness.

"Dawn is just breaking, Sire."

The King sat up and taking his arm from around Anastasia rose to his feet.

"I am ready to leave as soon as we can see the way."

"I would like to make a suggestion, Sire," Captain Aznar said.

"Of course," the King replied. "What is it?"

"We have been talking," Captain Aznar answered, "and we feel, Sire, it would be wisest for you to go on ahead to the Barracks without the Queen. We are, all of us, absolutely convinced that the Army is loyal and will do whatever you ask of them."

He paused and added,

"At the same time a revolutionary spirit has been engendered in the country and there might be some soldiers who would seize this opportunity to make trouble."

Captain Aznar paused to glance at Anastasia.

"We feel it would be safer if Her Majesty should join you later, Sire."

"I am sure you are right, Aznar," the King answered. "In fact there is no point in Her Majesty coming to the Barracks at all. I intend to rally the Army and lead them immediately along the coast road into Sergei. There I shall restore order and imprison or drive out of our country all the insurgents and revolutionaries."

The King spoke with a firmness and authority that made Anastasia look at him in surprise.

This was a very different man from the one who had felt so unhappy and humiliated the night before.

Here was a man who was prepared to lead and assert himself – here was a man ready to command and fight.

She rose from the blanket they had slept on and shook out the full skirts of her velvet riding habit.

"Where do you suggest, Sire, I should take Her Majesty?" Captain Aznar asked respectfully.

Anastasia felt from the sound of his voice that he too was surprised and relieved at the change in the King.

"The Palace of Huesca is not far from the Barracks," the King answered. "It has been shut up for years, but it is, I know, guarded by my father's own Dragoon Guards. If anyone is loyal to the Monarchy, it will be they."

"You are absolutely right, Sire!" Captain Aznar said respectfully. "The Dragoon Guards would die for the Crown and Her Majesty will be safe at the Palace."

"Take Her Majesty there, Aznar, and I will join you as soon as it is possible for me to do so."

Anastasia longed to cry out that she wanted to be with him and that she did not wish to be sent to safety.

She wanted to see him in action – she wanted to be there in case there should be another plot against his life, in case once again he should encounter treachery and betrayal.

But she knew that she would only be an encumbrance. He had a man's job to do and there was no place in it for a weak woman.

The King picked up his Cavalry cloak and threw it round his shoulders. Then he took his hat from where he had laid it down the night before and turned to Anastasia.

Captain Aznar had gone from the cave and they were alone.

The King looked at her in the flickering light of the candle that had nearly gutted out.

She had pushed back the white chiffon scarf from her head during the night and now her fair hair framed her pale face. Her blue eyes were wide and anxious as they looked up at the King.

"Take care of yourself, my beautiful wife," he sughed. "I shall be thinking of you, and behaving in a manner which I hope will make you proud of me."

Anastasia put out her hands towards him impulsively.

"You will not take unnecessary – risks?" she begged.

"I shall not run away from danger," he answered, "but I shall make every effort to return to you."

He smiled in a manner she found irresistible.

"I have not yet finished my battle where you are concerned," he said softly.

She looked up into his eyes and was very still. She thought for one moment that he might kiss her goodbye.

Then he bent his head and raised both her hands to his lips.

He kissed the backs of them before he turned them over and kissed the palms, first one and then the other.

His lips were warm and hard and somehow demanding and at the touch of them she felt the same sensation as when they lay close on the straw, streaking through her almost like a flash of lightning.

It was more intense, more thrilling than it had been before and her heart seemed to move into her throat so she could not speak.

Then, as the King released her and turned without another word to leave the cavern, she followed him, still aware of the pressure of his lips against her skin.

The King's horse was standing saddled outside the entrance to the cave and three Officers were mounted and waiting.

Only Captain Aznar was on foot and he held the bridle of the black stallion as the King picked up the reins and swung himself into the saddle.

"Take care of Her Majesty, Aznar," he said. "I am entrusting to you someone very precious."

"I am aware of that, Sire," Captain Aznar replied.

~ 195 ~

The King turned his head to look at Anastasia.

In the faint grey light of dawn she seemed like a spirit from another world against the darkness of the mountain behind her.

She might have been a spirit of spring coming up from the bowels of winter to bring the promise of hope and sunshine ahead.

For a moment the Kings eyes lingered on her face, until with what seemed an effort he spurred his horse and followed the three Officers who were already moving away.

With her hands clasped together, Anastasia stood watching.

She had a sudden terror that the King might be riding out of her life and as he disappeared into the grey mist and she could see him no more, she knew that she loved him.

It was nearly half an hour before Captain Aznar would agree to leave the caves and lead Anastasia over the mountaintop to start the descent on the other side.

By this time dawn had broken and the valley below them was suffused with sunshine, while the mountain mists were melting away with every second that passed.

As she waited, Anastasia could only think of the King.

She must have loved him, she thought, from the first moment she had seen him!

He had been so utterly different from what she had expected and his face had fascinated and enthralled her so that she had blurted out the first words that came into her mind.

And love, although she had not recognised it, had been growing within her every moment they had been together. She had never been in love before, so how could she have known that in those strange moments when it had been hard to breathe, when he had brought the colour flowing into her cheeks or made her heart seem to beat unaccountably fast, she had felt love?

Now it was all so obvious.

She loved him as she must have loved him on their wedding night, when she had asked him not to make love to her, as he had been ready to do.

Would things have been very different, she asked herself, if she had let him behave as a normal bridegroom rather than lie at her side, neither touching nor kissing her?

She felt herself thrill at the thought of his lips and she knew now that she wished inexpressibly that he had kissed her goodbye.

She felt a sudden panic sweep over her in case she never saw him again.

Suppose the revolutionaries killed him?

Suppose the Army would not follow him and instead took him prisoner and handed him over to the French?

Then she felt sure that she was torturing herself unnecessarily and she knew almost clairvoyantly that the King would win through and, as he intended, drive the French revolutionaries out of the country.

She had admired him before, but what she felt for him this morning after he had spoken with such authority and determination was a different kind of admiration.

Now at last, she told herself, he was in command of his own destiny, now he would rely not on his French friends, not on his Statesmen and Diplomatic advisers, but on himself.

He would make the decisions and he would conquer, as she wanted him to do.

"We can go now, ma'am," Captain Aznar piped up, breaking in on her thoughts.

Anastasia pulled her chiffon scarf over her head and allowed the Captain to help her into the saddle.

The air was still cold and crisp because they were so high up, but there was no need for her to wear the Cavalry cloak and Captain Aznar threw it over his own saddle.

"I shall leave the blanket behind, ma'am," he smiled. "Perhaps it will be of use to some stranded mountaineer."

"We might need it ourselves," Anastasia said, thinking that, if the revolutionaries were too strong for the Army, the King might have to flee for his life and once again they would be grateful for the shelter of the caves.

"You must not be afraid," Captain Aznar said as if he read her thoughts. "I have never known His Majesty to be as resolute as he was this morning."

"It was how you wanted him to be?" Anastasia asked.

"Exactly, ma'am! It is what we have all longed for and what the people have wanted for a long time."

"You are no longer – afraid of the – French?" Anastasia asked a little hesitatingly.

"I think if we are determined and, as the Emperor is well aware, we have England's protection, he will be deterred from openly taking an aggressive attitude against us."

"I understand. That was why their plot was so clever, to make the King himself ask them to intervene. It would have made it almost impossible for England to interfere."

"It is exactly as you say, ma'am," Captain Aznar agreed, "and now everything will be very different."

He paused and then added almost derisively,

"The Emperor fancies himself as another Napoleon Bonaparte, but he is nothing of the sort! I am convinced that sooner or later France will suffer defeat at the hands of the Prussians."

Anastasia looked at him in surprise.

"The Prussians?"

"Their ambition is boundless. Paris has always been a gaudy prize they have coveted."

When they reached the top of the mountain they could see that the descending paths were little more than a series of sheep tracks where the horses must tread warily – for one slip might mean a fall of hundreds, if not thousands of feet over sheer rock.

Anastasia looked down into the valley, hoping that she might catch a glimpse of the King and his escort.

But this side of the Pyrenees was far more rugged, and it was impossible to see for any distance until they had descended far lower down the mountainside.

Then the sun came out and it was hot.

The night before, Anastasia had been glad of her warm velvet riding habit. But now after they had been riding for an hour she regretted she was not wearing one of the fashionable summer habits of white pique or thin silk, a fashion which had been set in Paris by the ladies who rode in the *Bois de Boulogne*.

Finally, when they had left the mountains behind and had reached the valley, it was to find the terrain was very different from that around Sergei.

Here in addition to vines and olive groves, the vegetation was more profuse and more tropical.

There were palms, cactuses, the wild flowers seemed larger and more exotic and the brilliant butterflies were a delight to the eye.

Soon they came to trees heavy with oranges just turning to gold. Anastasia would have liked to stop and eat one, but she knew that Captain Aznar was in a hurry to reach the Palace.

Quite unexpectedly they came upon it standing high above a fertile valley and she thought how beautiful it was.

By this time she had learnt from Captain Aznar that, like the Alhambra in Granada, it had been built by the Moors who at one time had conquered this part of the country and the architecture they had left behind them was a lasting memorial to their Arab splendour.

The Huesca Palace was white with domes and spires that one could see from a long distance.

It was also surrounded by dark and tapering cypress trees, which gave it a mysterious appearance as they drew nearer. They climbed up to the outer gateway on a road Anastasia noted was badly in need of repair and, when they reached the iron gates surmounted by a crown, it was to find two sentries leaning against them, negligently talking to each other.

When they saw Captain Aznar approaching, they stared at first in surprise, then sprang to attention.

He drew his horse to a standstill and looked at them in a manner that Anastasia knew made them feel uncomfortable, and then he spoke sharply,

"I am Captain Aznar of His Majesty's Cavalry. Where is the Officer of the day?"

"He is in the Palace, sir," one of the soldiers answered.

"Open the gates!" Captain Aznar commanded.

The two sentries hurried to obey him and they rode through.

Now Anastasia could see the garden was a blaze of colour, with purple bougainvillaea rioting over the ancient walls. There were a number of fountains, which were not playing, and although the garden was well tended she had a feeling it had grown wild over the years and had not been trimmed back as it should have been.

The Palace, with its arcades of white marble, its latticework and arched windows, looked like something from the *Arabian Nights*.

It was, however, all very silent and quiet.

'The Palace of a *Sleeping Beauty*, who has not been awakened for a hundred years!' Anastasia thought.

When they reached the front door, she looked back far away into the valley and she realised that the Palace was magnificently situated and the view was breathtaking!

In the far distance she could see the faint blue of the sea and she wondered if the King had already reached the coast road and was riding at the head of his troops towards Sergei.

She felt a little tremor of fear for his safety and found herself praying for him, feeling in some mystical way that her prayers protected him and kept him safe.

Captain Aznar had dismounted to ring the bell and now an old servant wearing a threadbare livery, which should long ago have been replaced, opened the door.

"Who is in charge of the Palace?" Captain Azaar asked him firmly.

"There are only a few of us here, sir," the servant answered in a quivering voice, "but I will fetch the Major Domo."

"Fetch him!" Captain Aznar commanded, "and also the Officer of the day."

As he spoke, a man in uniform came from a room that was just inside the main entrance.

"What is all this?" he asked, "who are you and what do you want?"

"I am Captain Aznar of the King's Cavalry, escorting Her Majesty the Queen!"

The expression on the Officer's face was for a moment ludicrous.

His jaw literally dropped open, and then, as he came to attention, Captain Aznar assisted Anastasia from her horse.

"We did not know – we were not expecting you – ma'am," the Officer began.

"I know that," Anastasia answered. "Captain Aznar will explain to you the events that are taking place in Sergei. We are staying here until His Majesty joins us."

"His Majesty!" the Officer gasped.

With a smile Anastasia walked past him into the Palace.

Never had she realised that any place could be so entrancing.

In Moorish fashion the Palace was laid out in a series of courts. There was the Court of Myrtles, where orange-trees were reflected in a pool of green water and which seemed to her like a stanza of poetry.

The Court of the Dolphins was so beautiful that it might have been designed for Scheherazade.

There were arcades and horseshoe arches, oblong courtyards, projecting kiosks with long slender columns and everywhere the lace-like decoration of the purest white marble with fountains issuing from the mouths of leopards and dolphins.

How could anyone, Anastasia wondered, prefer a Palace that was an imitation of Versailles to this Fairyland of beauty?

She went to one of the windows to look out into the garden, which she could see was planted with cypresses, myrtle, oleanders and all manner of scented and flowering shrubs.

There was the red, purple and white of flowering geraniums, the pink, crimson and flame of carnations, while the fountains and statues all had an enchantment about them that was unlike anything Anastasia had ever seen before.

'No one could live here,' she told herself, 'and not wish to be beautiful. No one could look on such beauty and not think beautiful thoughts.'

She walked back the way she had come to find Captain Aznar giving instructions to a bewildered staff.

They were mostly very old men and women who had lived in the Palace all their lives and had served a King they seldom saw and of whom they heard little.

"Are you opening the whole Palace?" Anastasia asked.

"Would that be your wish, ma'am?" Captain Aznar enquired.

"Let us open it," Anastasia said eagerly, "let us make it look as it used to."

She looked at the old servants and said quietly,

"You must find some younger people to help you. There will be girls and men in the villages who, I am sure, would be glad to come and work in the Palace. You can instruct them and we can make Huesca a place where His Majesty will be happy."

She knew that her words had excited their imagination. When they were dismissed, she heard them chattering like a whole colony of budgerigars, as they hurried away to throw open the closed shutters, pull the dustsheets off the furniture, and make the 'Queen's Room' ready for her.

The room, when she reached it, was far more beautiful than her room in the Palace at Sergei.

Here there was no great canopied bed weighted down with carving and curtained with silk and velvet.

Instead the low headboard, of a Moorish type, was a shell of mother-of-pearl. It gleamed as if it had just risen from the sea, and was supported by mermaids and dolphins carved in alabaster.

The furniture in the room with its marble latticework and domed ceiling echoed the theme of the ocean and the curtains were of coral gauze embroidered with silver.

"It is all so lovely!" Anastasia said to Captain Aznar. "A Palace of dreams!"

"It is a dream come true that you should be here, ma'am."

"Do you think the people in this part of the country will feel that?" she asked.

"I know they will," he replied.

Would the King think she was like a dream? She felt she would know if she looked into his eyes, what he really thought of her.

Then she remembered how hard it had been at times to keep her eyes on his, how his expression had made her blush, how occasionally he gave her a mocking and quizzical look which made her feel very young and immature.

There was so much for her to learn, so much to understand and she felt it would be possible only if the King came to love her.

"Make him love me God! Please – *please* – make him love me," she whispered.

She thought there was a note of hope in the song of the birds in the sun-kissed and fragrant garden.

Later in the day Anastasia was told that there was a crowd outside the gates and the sentries had been reinforced.

But the local peasants were only standing and staring at the Palace as if they would ascertain for themselves the truth of the rumour of the Queen's arrival.

Anastasia could see from the windows that many of them held in their hands small bunches of flowers.

"I am going to look at the people outside," she said to Captain Aznar.

She saw the surprise in his eyes, but he said nothing and only followed her as she went down the steps of the Palace and out into the sunshine.

It was so warm that she had discarded her riding coat and wore only her full velvet skirt and a soft white muslin blouse inset with lace.

She had no hat, so over her head she carried a white sunshade that she had found in an umbrella stand. It had yellowed with age and might have belonged to the King's mother or one of her Ladies-in-Waiting.

Anastasia lifted it over her head and walked towards the gates.

The sentries came to attention.

"Please open the gates," Anastasia said.

"Do you wish to go outside, ma'am?" Captain Aznar asked in a surprised voice.

"I wish to talk with my visitors," Anastasia replied with a smile.

She could see they were peasants, most of them dressed in their national costume, many of them holding a child by the hand and with another in their arms.

All of them were poor, but attractive with their dark eyes, black hair and soft olive skin that looked as if it had been coloured by the golden sun.

As Anastasia drew near, they suddenly realised who she was and gave a nervous, somewhat hesitating cheer.

Then, as the gates opened, they parted and moved sideways as if they expected her to walk past them.

When she stopped and started to talk – first to an old woman and then to a younger one to ask the age of a child, to question a man about the work he did – they stared at her incredulously.

Then, as she went on talking to them one after another in their own language, their confidence grew and they began to offer her the flowers they held in their hands.

Soon Anastasia's arms were full and Captain Aznar was accepting flowers on her behalf until he too could carry no more and was forced to hand them over to a soldier.

At last, after she had talked and walked among them for nearly an hour, Anastasia turned to go.

There was no doubt then about the cheers that rang out and seemed to echo amongst the trees, for they were so spontaneous and so warm-hearted.

They called after her, cheering and shouting until finally she reached the Palace and disappeared inside.

"That was a wonderful thing to have done, ma'am," Captain Aznar said. "It has never happened before that a Queen has actually moved amongst her people without formality and without protocol."

"It is something that must happen again," Anastasia insisted firmly.

Then, as if she suddenly realised how long she had been in the Palace, she walked to the window to look down into the valley.

"How far are the Barracks from here?" she asked.

"About six miles, ma'am."

"Is it possible for us to find out what is happening?"

"I instructed the Officer of the day as soon as I arrived to send an Officer on horseback to Leziga," Captain Aznar replied. "He was to inform His Majesty that you had arrived safely and also to wait for any message that His Majesty might wish to send in return."

"Thank you," Anastasia said. "It is so hard – not to – worry."

"I understand, ma'am, but I am sure that everything will be all right."

"How can we be sure of anything," Anastasia asked, "until we learn what sort of reception His Majesty receives in Sergei?"

Captain Aznar did not answer and Anastasia felt a fear that had been lurking behind her all day creeping up insidiously, as if it was a serpent slithering into this Eden she had found so unexpectedly.

She was afraid, desperately afraid, because she loved the King and because she knew she wanted more than she had ever wanted anything in her life for him to come back to her.

Then, as if the serpent struck at her, she remembered that while she might be in love with him, he was certainly not in love with her.

He loved the Comtesse, and although he knew her now to be a traitor who had abused his affection, there was no reason to think that he could transfer his affections so quickly to herself.

They had talked of love, that was true, but he had never said that he loved her.

How could she ever be sure, she wondered, that it was not just a matter of politics for him to have his wife desperately in love with him? To ensure that because of her affection they had children – the son who was so essential as heir to the throne?

She felt as if such thoughts destroyed the very beauty of the Palace and yet she could not suppress them.

They crept upon her questioning, suggesting, insinuating and, because she knew there was some substance of truth in each one of them, she could not escape from the poison they exuded.

'I love him! I love him!' she thought despairingly.

She wondered unhappily if he would ever love her and whether they would find together the *'fire of love'* he had described to her so eloquently.

*

Anastasia went upstairs before dinner to bathe in a bath sunk in a marble floor. The walls were decorated with exquisite mosaics set with semi-precious quartz, and there were urns carved from transparent alabaster.

It was sad that she had nothing to put on except her riding clothes and in a way she was glad that the King was not there because she thought she would not look attractive enough for him.

The old housemaid who attended her had already procured a young girl from the village to help and was instructing her.

The girl stared at Anastasia with an unmistakable look of admiration in her dark eyes and somehow that in itself was vaguely comforting.

Anastasia had lunched alone, but she told Captain Aznar he must dine with her.

"Shall I also ask the Officer of the day?" she enquired.

"I understand, ma'am, that as a matter of routine a Senior Officer is expected to arrive late tonight with a troop of Dragoon Guards from Leziga Barracks to relieve the Guards now on duty. I think it would be wiser for you to wait until tomorrow."

Anastasia smiled.

"You think there might be jealousy if a junior Officer was entertained before his senior?"

"Soldiers are men, ma'am, and I think you have given the Officer of the day enough excitement for the moment."

Anastasia laughed.

Then her smile faded and she asked,

"There is no message from Leziga?"

"Not yet, ma'am, but I am expecting word at any moment"

Dinner was a simple meal, which Anastasia thoroughly enjoyed. It consisted only of local produce. There was blue trout fresh from a mountain stream and wild guinea fowl she had seen flying through the trees as they descended the mountain, their high shrill voices cackling to each other and scaring the other birds.

Wild strawberries – *fraises de bois* – followed, sweet and succulent. She had also seen them growing in the woods, their little red heads peeping beneath their pretty green leaves.

"The chef is very apologetic that this is the best he can provide tonight," Captain Aznar said.

"Will you please reassure him and say that I have enjoyed the meal immensely. It is the best dinner I have had since I came to Maurona," Anastasia replied. "I shall never forget how long drawn out and exhausting the Wedding Banquet was. I thought it would never come to an end!"

Captain Aznar laughed.

"Most people, ma'am, fast for several days before they embark upon a State Banquet! There is always too much to be eaten by too few!"

Coffee was brought to the table in beautiful Moorish cups, handleless and set in gold holders decorated with coral and turquoises.

"How pretty!" Anastasia exclaimed.

"His late Majesty collected many Moorish and Arabic treasures in the Palace," Captain Aznar explained. "Tomorrow when all the rooms are open I think you will find much to interest you, ma'am."

"I am sure I shall," Anastasia answered.

Then the words were arrested on her lips as a servant came into the room.

He bent his head and spoke to Captain Aznar.

"The Officer has arrived from Leziga with news, ma'am. Would you wish to see him?"

"Yes, of course."

It was difficult to conceal her impatience as the servant went from the room to return a few moments later with a young Officer wearing the uniform of the Dragoon Guards.

He saluted smartly and stood just inside the door waiting to be spoken to.

"What has happened?" Anastasia asked impulsively. "Is His Majesty safe?"

She could not prevent the words sounding frantic or hide her anxiety.

"His Majesty arrived early this morning, ma'am," the Officer answered. "The troops at Leziga were immediately paraded in front of him. He informed them of his plans and they set off for Sergei."

"How did they go?" Anastasia asked.

"The Cavalry went first, ma'am, His Majesty leading them. The cannons and lighter guns drawn by horses followed with the foot soldiers marching behind."

"Have you heard anything of what has happened?" Anastasia enquired.

"His Majesty commanded me to stay with him until he could send a message back containing the information he felt you, ma'am, would wish to hear."

"What was it? Tell me!" Anastasia commanded.

The Officer drew a piece of paper from his pocket. "His Majesty's note is brief," he said and read aloud –

"There was opposition in the environs of the City, but this was overcome with some casualties on both sides. The Revolutionaries are now in the process of being rounded up. There are small pockets of resistance in some areas and snipers on many of the buildings."

"Is that – all?" Anastasia asked in a small voice.

"I waited in case there should be a second message," the Officer replied, "but I thought Your Majesty might be anxious, so I came here as quickly as I could."

"Thank you very much. I am sure you must be hungry and need a drink. Captain Aznar will look after you."

The Officers went from the room and Anastasia walked out into the Court of the Dolphins. The night was warm and the air fragrant with the scent of flowers.

The fountains had been turned on and now the water was being thrown high into the sky to fall again into an exquisitely carved basin with a soft tinkling sound, otherwise there was only silence.

It was an immeasurable relief to know that the revolution was over. At the same time Anastasia knew that it might easily break out again.

Perhaps the insurgents were reorganising their forces, perhaps they were waiting for nightfall to strike again. Apart from this, she had hoped, perhaps foolishly, for a personal message from the King, something he would say to her alone, something to tell her that he was thinking of her.

Then she told herself she was asking too much. Besides, he could have no idea how much she longed to hear from him.

She thought now how stupid she had been not to have let him know clearly before he went away that she loved him and then remembered she had not really known it herself.

He probably thought she was still indifferent – or perhaps cold, as he believed all English women were.

Did he really wish to win the personal battle of which he had spoken? Did he really want her with the same strange, unpredictable ache within his heart that she felt when she thought of him?

"I want him! I want him!" she whispered to the fountain.

It seemed as if her hopes rose like the water into the sky, only to fall defeated into the pool below.

How long she stayed in the Court of the Dolphins she had no idea.

She only felt as if she was giving out herself to the man she loved, sending a winged message right from her very heart and soul towards him – wherever he might be.

Once when they had been together she had felt, although he did not move and did not touch her, as if he was drawing her towards him.

Now she felt as if she was drawing him, praying for him, longing for him, wanting him with her whole being, so that it seemed impossible that he should not be aware of it.

Then again, within her mind, like the rustle of a serpent, came the thought of the Comtesse with her fascinating provocative face, her inviting lips and sensuous eyes!

Despairingly, Anastasia thought that the King could never feel for her what he had felt for a woman so alluring.

She had made the King believe that he must woo her mind, but at this moment it was not her mind that ached for him! It was not her mind that had felt that strange exciting thrill when he had pressed his lips on her palm.

It was not her mind that had moved nearer to him so that their bodies touched as they lay together in the cold cave.

'I want him to love me! Oh, God – I want him to love me!' Anastasia prayed. 'Even if it is not the sort of wonderful and all-consuming fire he spoke about, I will be grateful for anything he will give me – anything!'

She felt as if her prayer winged its way into the sky high above her head.

Then, slowly, she moved back through the labyrinth of marble passages and mounted the carved staircase to her lonely bedroom.

Chapter Eight

'I have been here for five days,' Anastasia told herself as she stood looking out over the valley.

She hoped that she would see soldiers riding along the dusty narrow road leading to the Palace and that one of them might be the King.

'If he does not send for me tomorrow,' she thought, 'I will go to him, whatever he may think about it.'

Every day there had been bulletins from Sergei brought to her in the evening by an Officer, but they had merely been brief military reports of what had occurred.

As Anastasia had feared, the insurgents had regrouped themselves and there had been fierce fighting in some parts of the City and round the Palace.

The third day after she had been at Huesca, Olivia had arrived in an Army wagon with an escort of soldiers and trunks filled with her gowns.

Captain Aznar had ushered her into the room where Anastasia was sitting.

"A visitor to see you, ma'am," he said with a smile, "who I know will be welcome."

Anastasia looked round, then sprang to her feet.

"Olivia!" she exclaimed, "I was hoping you would come!"

"His Majesty arranged it," Olivia replied, "and I have brought many of Your Majesty's gowns with me."

"That is what I have longed for," Anastasia sighed and then in a more serious voice asked, "what is happening in Sergei?"

It was Olivia who told her far more than the King's bulletins had done.

She related how the revolution had started with the firing of guns, crowds of people yelling and shouting in the streets, and setting fire to a number of houses in the poorer quarters of the City.

Those were the flames, Anastasia realise, that she and the King had seen as they rode up the side of the mountain.

"At first there was a great deal of confusion in the Palace," Olivia explained, "because no one knew what was happening. Then the Chamberlain and the other officials came to find His Majesty. I explained that you had both left for Leziga."

"What did the Palace officials think of that?" Anastasia asked.

"They were surprised, Your Majesty, but as the noise outside grew more insistent they realised it had been a sensible move."

"Go on!" Anastasia urged.

"The crowds – obviously incited to do so – screamed outside the Palace gates, *'down with the Monarchy!'* and shouted disrespectful things about His Majesty."

Anastasia had no desire to know what these were, so she merely waited for Olivia to continue.

"They started firing through the gates and it was all rather frightening. Then, later in the day, when we realised that the Army was marching along the coast road, everything seemed to change."

"In what way?" Anastasia asked.

"I think, Your Majesty, a number of people did not believe me when I said the King had gone to Leziga. They thought that you had both gone to France."

"How could they believe that His Majesty would do anything so disloyal of his own free will?" Anastasia asked angrily.

Then she realised that it would be an obvious theory, considering how friendly the King was meant to be with the Emperor and how strong the French influence was in Sergei.

"Pedro and I went to the top of the Palace, Your Majesty," Olivia continued. "We could see our troops advancing and hear the gunfire and see the revolutionaries being driven back."

"They had arms and weapons?" Anastasia asked.

"All of French origin," Olivia answered, "all of the very latest design! Pedro overheard the soldiers in the Palace talking about it."

Anastasia gave a little sigh.

"They were defeated?"

"By His Majesty!" Olivia cried, "and, when he rode at the head of his troops into the centre of the City, everyone cheered him!

"That was a dangerous thing to do," Anastasia exclaimed. "He could easily have been shot by a sniper or by someone in the crowd."

"We all recognised that, but there is nothing Mauronians admire more than a man who is brave and not afraid of danger."

She clasped her hands together.

"Pedro and I, Your Majesty, were in the Market Place. When the King spoke to us, we were at first proud and then because what he said was so moving, we were all in tears."

"What did His Majesty say?" Anastasia asked anxiously.

"He promised the mistakes of the past would all be rectified and he pledged himself to make Maurona, with our help, a free and prosperous country."

There were tears in Olivia's eyes, as if just to remember the emotions the King had aroused brought back vividly her feeling of pride and patriotism.

Anastasia wished she had been there.

She could visualise how magnificent the King must have looked and she was sure, without being told, that the new aura of authority and leadership he seemed to develop after the night in the cave would have been very impressive.

That, she had told him, was what his people wanted. That was what they had longed for over the years and there could be no doubt now that they would follow him.

It had been a joy, once Olivia had arrived, to change from the velvet riding habit of which she was heartily tired and put on one of the pretty gowns with its large crinoline she had brought with her from London.

She had seen the admiration in the womens' eyes when she had, as usual, gone out after luncheon through the Palace gates to walk amongst the crowds that assembled there every day.

More and more people came, some from villages high up in the Pyrenees – so far that they had to start their journey before sunrise so as to reach the Palace in time for her appearance.

It had been difficult to know what to do with so many floral tributes she received every afternoon and because she knew they were given to her with affection she could not bear to throw them away.

Finally she instructed two of the village girls to make them into potpourri and big bowls of sweet fragrant flower petals began to appear everywhere in the Palace.

She noticed that the sentries had been trebled on the gate and, when she questioned Captain Aznar about it, he replied,

"The Officer in Command of the Dragoons, ma'am, does not approve of your taking such risks."

"Can he possibly think I am in danger from these gentle peasants?" Anastasia asked.

"There is always the chance, ma'am, that a stranger might slip in amongst them. By now it will be known in Sergei where you are staying."

Sure enough, the following afternoon there was an incident that might have proved disastrous had it not been for the alertness of Captain Aznar.

As Anastasia went through the gates, there appeared to be an even larger crowd than usual waiting.

They looked very colourful. The women's predominantly red skirts worn with black bodices and white embroidered blouses, the children with bright ribbons in their hair and the flowers that nearly all of them held in their hands, made it seem like a festival.

Anastasia found it slightly embarrassing that many of the mothers asked her to bless their children.

"How can I do such a thing?" she had asked Captain Aznar once she understood what they requested.

"These people believe in the Divine Right of Kings, ma'am," Captain Aznar replied, "and as Your Majesty is so exquisitely beautiful, kind and compassionate, already they believe you to be a Saint!"

Anastasia looked at him in surprise as if she thought he was joking. Then she saw the expression in his eyes that told her that he felt very much the same about her as the peasants outside.

More than once she was surprised at the adoration in his expression when they were talking together and she knew that when he had said he would not only die for her, but live for her, it had been an irrevocable vow.

Anastasia was talking to a woman who had five children, four of whom could walk. She had brought them many miles to see their Queen, and the fifth child, a baby of only two months old, she had carried in her arms.

"Bless them, Your Majesty, bless them!" she begged, "so that they will be lucky all through their lives."

"I am sure they will be lucky in having a mother who loves them," Anastasia replied.

But because she knew it would make this simple woman happy, she touched the children on their heads and hoped that the little prayer she said for them would not seem blasphemous.

Just as she turned to move away to speak to someone else in the crowd, she saw a man on the outskirts make a sudden movement with his arm.

She hardly had time to think that he might be doing something strange before Captain Aznar had put his arms round her and pulled her down on to the ground.

A shot rang out deafeningly.

There was a scream from the crowd, followed by a roar of anger, and the soldiers reached the man only just in time to prevent him from being torn to pieces.

Captain Aznar helped Anastasia to her feet.

"Are you all right?" he asked with a deep note of concern in his voice.

"I am all right," Anastasia answered a little shakily.

The women surged towards her, crying out in their anxiety, kneeling down to touch the hem of her skirt, exclaiming at the shame that had come amongst them that anyone should have tried to hurt their Queen.

"It is all right," Anastasia said, her voice ringing out above the noise.

"You must go back to the Palace, ma'am," Captain Aznar insisted.

"I have not talked to half the people," Anastasia replied, "and the danger has now passed. Please ask them to calm down and be quiet. I do not wish to leave them."

Her assailant had been hurried away and Anastasia was to learn later that he had been taken to Sergei to await trial.

"There might be another attempt on your life, ma'am," Captain Aznar persisted in a very low voice so that only Anastasia could hear him.

"I think it unlikely," Anastasia replied. "If there were other men here intending to kill me, they will have run away by now."

Despite Captain Aznar's protests, she insisted on remaining the full hour she had allotted herself to move amongst the people.

It was only when she at last returned to the Palace that she felt a little shaken, realising how near she had been to death.

'What would the King have thought if he learnt that I was dead?' she asked herself.

Would he have minded, as she would mind if he was killed? Or would he be relieved that he need no longer be encumbered by a bride whom Queen Victoria had chosen for him?

It was hard to think that he might have felt like that and yet, Anastasia told herself, there was always the possibility of it.

*

The second day after she had arrived at the Palace, carriages came driving up the unkept roadway carrying members of the distinguished Mauronian families who lived in the vicinity.

They had expected simply to leave their names in the official visitors' book, which stands in the hall of every Palace, and then drive away.

To their surprise, however, Anastasia received them in person – and even more to their surprise, they found themselves sitting down comfortably with the Queen and enjoying a cup of tea.

Never in the stiff protocol that had governed everything in the days of His Late Majesty had such a thing happened.

What was more, the new Queen not only laughed and talked in an easy manner that made them feel at home, but she also seemed insatiably curious about their part of the realm, which they had thought for many years was of no interest to those who lived in Sergei.

The first-comers left both astonished and captivated by Anastasia, and what they had to say about her brought an increasing number of their friends and neighbours on the following days.

"I think, ma'am," Captain Aznar said, "it would be wise for you to choose some Ladies-in-Waiting from among the noble families who have come here to pay their respects."

For the first time Anastasia refused to consider one of his suggestions.

"No!" she said firmly.

"It will cause surprise and comment, ma'am, if you do not have Ladies-in-Waiting in attendance."

"I do not care!" Anastasia answered. "They can say what they like, but I am not setting up a Court without His Majesty's permission and then only after he has joined me here."

She spoke so positively that Captain Aznar was silent.

Anastasia knew that he was wise in what he had suggested. At the same time she was determined that, when the King came to her, she would not be cluttered by the formality of attendants.

She wanted to be alone with him.

She wanted, if such an idea was possible, to spend part of their honeymoon here.

He had spoken of taking her to a villa near the sea and she remembered he had also said it was near the French border. She had wondered at the time if he had chosen that villa because it was near his friends.

Would he want to stay with her at Huesca?

Would he feel, as she did, that the beautiful Moorish rooms, the ancient courtyards and the tropical gardens were a perfect setting for love?

She felt a little thrill run through her at the thought.

Then she remembered that the King did not love her, and where she was enchanted, perhaps he would notice only that much of the Palace needed repairing and parts of it were definitely shabby.

'Perhaps what is seen with the eyes is really what is felt in the heart,' Anastasia thought and longed to ask the King if that were true.

There were so many things she wanted to talk to him about, so many questions she wished to ask him, and she kept remembering their conversations on the first day after their wedding.

In retrospect it seemed a golden day of sunshine and happiness.

That was what she felt – for him it might mean something different.

Now to Anastasia every hour that the King did not come to her seemed to be long, drawn out and empty.

At times she wanted him with an intensity that frightened her.

At night, as she lay in the big bed beneath the mother-of-pearl shell, she would hear the nightingales singing in the garden below and feel that the beauty of the starlit night was wasted because she was alone.

She found herself thinking of how the King had lain beside her the first night they were married and promised he would not touch her.

She knew that, if he was here now, she would want him to touch her, in fact she would ask him to do so.

Merely to think of it made her quiver with that same feeling that had been hers when he kissed the palms of her hands.

"*I love him*!" Anastasia cried aloud.

She wondered how many other women had slept in this marble and alabaster chamber and whispered the same words into the scented night.

"If the King does not come tomorrow, I shall go to him!"

She said the same words over and over to herself all through the day.

She talked to the crowds outside the gate.

There were over a dozen people who called to have tea with her, people she liked and with whom she wanted to be friends.

With proud, clear-cut features and dark, intelligent eyes which were part of their Spanish heritage, many of them bore names that went far back into the history of both countries.

Anastasia could not help contrasting them with the people she had met in Sergei.

If she had been prejudiced against the French before, she found it hard now to think of those who favoured the enemies of Maurona without hating them.

It would be difficult in future, she thought, not to show her dislike, and she was determined that when finally she chose the Ladies of her Household, they would all come from this part of the country.

After dinner the usual Officer arrived from Sergei with his Official Bulletin.

"The City is now quiet. There have been no outbreaks of violence for over twenty-four hours. Parliament is in session and the Prime Minister, in consultation with His Majesty the King, has made a number of changes in the Cabinet."

Anastasia felt her heart leap with gladness.

The King was not only leading his Army but he was also asserting his control over the country as a whole!

She was sure, completely sure, that the changes meant that the French sympathisers would be dismissed from the seats of power and true Mauronians would be put in their places.

She knew that Captain Aznar was thinking the same thing and, when the messenger had left, she turned to him with a smile.

"Everything you have ever wanted, Captain, is coming true."

"Entirely due to you, ma'am."

"Perhaps the King would have been saved without – me," Anastasia said humbly.

"Who else would have found out about the plot to kidnap him?" Captain Aznar asked. "Who else would have sent for me so quickly that we had time to spirit His Majesty away safely?"

"I like to think I – saved him," Anastasia murmured.

"I think you have done that in more ways than one," Captain Aznar responded.

Anastasia knew exactly what he meant, but she could not help wondering if the King would be as grateful as his servants. After all, as a result of the French plot he would be forced to be rid of the Comtesse.

The previous day the King's Bulletin had ended with the words,

"All French residents, including the Ambassador of His Imperial Majesty, Napoleon III, have been asked to leave Maurona. They may subsequently apply for permission to re-enter the country, should they wish to do so!"

This measure had taken Anastasia and Captain Aznar by surprise, and when the Officer who had conveyed it from Sergei had read it out to them, they had at first hardly taken in its full significance.

It had been so poignant and personal where Anastasia was concerned that she had not been able to discuss it even after the messenger had left.

Instead she had merely bade Captain Aznar goodnight and retired to her bedroom.

She had been overwhelmingly glad that the King had taken so firm a step. At the same time she could not help wondering what he personally felt about it.

Could he really bear never to see the Comtesse again? Or was he already planning that sooner or later he would visit Paris, where they could meet, perhaps secretly?

She could hardly credit that he would stoop to such subterfuge, but at the same time she knew now that, when in love, nothing really mattered except the person who held the strings of one's heart.

She knew that in her own case, even if the King was the most dangerous enemy England had ever had, she would love him no less overwhelmingly.

She would still try to see him and she would still long to be close to him.

Would not the King, she asked herself, feel the same about the fascinating Comtesse le Granmont?

Now Captain Aznar broke in on her thoughts.

"If there is nothing else I can do for you, ma'am, I will bid you goodnight. Perhaps tomorrow we shall hear from His Majesty."

"Do you think he will soon be – free to come – here?" Anastasia asked in a small voice.

"It is obvious, ma'am, that His Majesty has been very busy in Sergei, reconstructing the whole constitution. Perhaps he will ask you to go to him?"

"I understand from Olivia that there has been some damage done to the Palace," Anastasia answered.

"I have heard that too, but it may be merely superficial and the Palace quite habitable."

"I thought perhaps His Majesty might have mentioned it in his Bulletin."

"I should imagine it can be speedily repaired," Captain Aznar remarked.

Without thinking Anastasia exclaimed.

"Oh, I hope not!"

He looked at her in surprise and she explained,

"I want to stay here!"

She saw the delight in his expression and added,

"That is something that would please you, would it not?"

"You know it would, ma'am, and I think the whole country would appreciate it too. But I doubt if you could persuade His Majesty to agree."

"I shall try," Anastasia said firmly, "I promise you, I shall try. I love this Palace."

"If you will allow me to say so, ma'am, it is a worthy setting for your beauty."

She heard the deep note in Captain Aznar's voice that she recognised, but she did not answer him and after a moment he bowed formally and went from the room leaving her alone.

'He is so true and loyal!' Anastasia thought to herself.

She knew that he loved her, but it was a selfless, dedicated love and he would never speak of it. It was immeasurably comforting to know that he was there, and to realise how much he had helped her to an understanding of Maurona and its people.

She walked from the sitting room into the Court of the Dolphins.

There was the soft tinkle of falling water in the basin of the fountain and she looked up to where the stars were very bright in the darkness of the sky.

The fragrance of the flowers was overwhelming and because the beauty of it all made her feel restless,

Anastasia walked back into the sitting room and crossed it to one of the windows overlooking the valley.

She pulled back the curtains and opened wide the casements to look out.

The moonlight gave the valley a strange, mystical appearance, so that it seemed ethereal and part of a spirit world.

Down below her, proceeding along the road that was like a ribbon of silver in the moonlight, she suddenly saw horses.

They were travelling at a great pace and after a little while she could distinguish that there were six men riding two abreast at what appeared to be a phenomenal speed.

She was sure they were soldiers and suddenly she felt afraid.

Why were they in such a hurry? What had happened? What news were they bringing?

She watched them until they rounded the hill on which the Palace was built and were out of sight.

Now she knew they would be climbing the road up to the gates.

She wanted to ring for Captain Aznar, but found herself unable to move.

She felt as if the fear within her had sapped her will and left her unable to make a decision.

Supposing someone at the last moment had killed the King, even as a man had tried to kill her?

Supposing he was wounded – dying, and that was why the horsemen were galloping to bring her the news? Perhaps to convey her back to Sergei?

She stood waiting, immobile. She could only wait and listen with an anxiety that made it hard to breathe.

There was nothing but silence. Then, when she felt she must scream, because no one had come to her, the door opened.

For a moment, because of the very intensity of her feelings, Anastasia felt she could not see who stood there.

Then, as he came further into the room, she saw it was *the King*!

She gave a cry, which came from the very depths of her heart and yet somehow it was strangled in her throat so that it was a very small sound.

She could only stand staring at him, her eyes very large in her pale face.

The King was in uniform and his boots were dusty.

As Anastasia looked at him, she thought she had never seen him look so happy, so handsome or so vital.

There was a remarkable change in his appearance, which vaguely in her mind she recognised as a new aura of authority and self-assurance.

At last he spoke and his voice was very deep and low.

"Anastasia!

"You have come! I have been waiting! I have been so – afraid! You are not – hurt?"

"I promised you that I would take care of myself."

"From what I have – heard, you did – nothing of the sort!" Anastasia answered. "They have not – harmed you?"

"I am unharmed."

He came a little nearer to her and it seemed to Anastasia as if they were saying one thing with their lips but what vibrated on the air between them was something very different.

The King almost reached her and then he stopped.

He was looking at her in her wide crinoline silhouetted against the open window, at her bare neck and arms, at her hair shining in the lights, her wide eyes and her lips, trembling a little because of the surging excitement she felt at his sudden appearance.

"You are very beautiful, Anastasia!" he sighed at length. "More beautiful even than I remembered."

"You have – thought about – me?"

"All the time."

"I think you must have – known," she said in a voice that was hardly above a whisper, "that I was thinking of you – praying for you and – sending my prayers across the mountains to – protect you."

"I felt you near me while we were fighting," the King answered.

"I was sure you would win," Anastasia said, "but at the same time I was afraid, desperately afraid – especially just now when I saw you in the valley. I thought perhaps – because you were riding so fast, that messengers were coming to tell me you had been wounded – or killed."

"And now you know I am neither?"

"I am glad – more glad than I can tell you! It has been so – lonely and – empty here without you."

"You felt lonely without me?"

"Very – lonely!"

She looked into his eyes.

~ 233 ~

She saw a fire smouldering there and thought he would take her in his arms.

But almost abruptly he turned away.

"I want to talk to you, Anastasia," he said, and she thought his voice was unexpectedly harsh.

"What is – it?" she asked. "What has happened?"

A sudden desperate fear sprang into her mind that he was anxious to be rid of her and she felt a pain in her heart as if a dagger had pierced it.

The thought made her tremble and because he walked away from her across the room to the archway leading into the Court of the Dolphins she moved after him.

"What has happened? What is wrong?" she asked. "Is it something I have – done?"

"No, Anastasia. Everything you have done has been right and perfect! I have been told how you talk with the peasants at the gates, how you nearly lost your life in doing so. How could you have taken such a risk when you belong to me?"

"Captain Aznar saved me," Anastasia answered. "I thought perhaps you would decorate him for what he did."

"I owe more to Aznar than can be expressed by any decoration, but for the moment I am concerned only with you. Already the whole country is talking about you, Anastasia."

"You are not angry that I should have done anything so – unconventional?"

"I am proud – *very proud*!" the King answered.

"Then what have you to tell me? I am – afraid."

"What frightens you?"

Anastasia did not reply and after a moment he asked, "Tell me – I want to know."

"I am – frightened that you do not – want me any – more," Anastasia said in a very small voice.

He turned to look at her and after one quick glance at him she found it impossible to meet his eyes.

"What I have to say to you, Anastasia," the King said very quietly, "is that we cannot go on as we were before all this happened,"

"Why not?" Anastasia asked. "What do you mean? I don't – understand."

"The night we married," the King replied, "I gave you my promise that I would not kiss you or touch you until you asked me to do so. I meant to keep that promise, Anastasia. You told me I must woo your mind and that is what I was determined to do."

Anastasia clasped her hands together.

She realised he was speaking in the past tense and she was trembling.

"But now," the King went on, "I cannot keep that promise. That first night, while you were asleep I realised not only how lovely you are but also that you are everything a man could long for and desire."

Anastasia felt a thrill run through her as the King continued,

"Then the night in the cave when you put your arms around me, you not only comforted and sustained me, you also inspired me. I knew then that I love you as I have never loved a woman before."

Now Anastasia drew in her breath and her eyes were raised to the King's.

"Ever since then," he said, "I have never ceased thinking about you. You are with me in everything I think and in everything I do."

He paused before he continued,

"All during the fighting these past days I have found myself asking what you would think of as right, trying to behave always in a manner which I hoped would make you proud of me. You are so young, Anastasia, so innocent, so inexperienced in the ways of the world. And yet you have filled my whole life and now I know I am nothing unless I can gain your love."

He turned away from her as abruptly as he had done before to look at the fountain in the courtyard.

"I am frightened of destroying the trust you have in me," he said in a strange voice, "but it is because I love you unbearably, Anastasia, that I cannot go on as I intended, trying to win your mind and pretending that your body does not attract me to the point of madness!"

His voice deepened as he added,

"I am not an Englishman, I am from the sun. I tried to explain to you that love for me is an all-consuming fire which I cannot control!"

There was a silence during which Anastasia could not speak.

It seemed to her as if the whole room was lit with golden light.

She could not move – she could hardly breathe –

And then the King said,

"That is why I have come to tell you tonight that you must ask me to stay as your husband or else I must leave you immediately!"

The King made a sound that was half a laugh and half a groan.

"There is no question, my beautiful one, of lying beside you on the bed and playing at our pretence of marriage. I know that I cannot even stay under the same roof without touching you, without making you mine! I want you – God knows, *I want you!*"

His voice died away.

Then he said almost sharply,

"The choice is yours! If you tell me to go back to Sergei, I will obey you! But I beg you to release me from the promise I made you and allow me to show you the depth and reality of my love for you."

As the King was standing looking at the courtyard, it seemed as if the passion in his voice echoed through the marble latticework and became part of the music of the fountain.

Anastasia was trembling and she had locked her small fingers together so tightly that the knuckles showed white.

She knew that he was waiting for her answer and she knew what she wanted to say, but somehow the words would not come.

Then in a very shy little voice which was in complete contrast to the positiveness of his, she whispered,

"That night in the cave you said – you wanted to throw away your – decorations. I have thought that when you – came back to me I would like to – give you one more."

"Yes, of course, if that is your wish," the King replied.

She knew that his response was indifferent and that he imagined she was trying to change the subject.

"The decoration I would – give you," Anastasia said in a voice he could hardly hear, "is called – *'a Kiss for the King'*!"

For a moment he did not move.

Then he turned around and she saw the light in his eyes that transformed his whole face.

"Do you mean that?" he asked. "Oh, my precious little wife, do you really mean that?"

Anastasia was trembling but she lifted her face to his.

Very slowly, as if he fought for self-control, he put his arms round her and looked down into her face.

"I have dreamt of this," he said hoarsely, and his mouth took possession of hers.

For a moment he was gentle, then, as he felt Anastasia's lips respond to his, as he felt a thrill like quicksilver run through her and she pressed herself even closer against him, his kisses were fierce and demanding, passionate and insistent.

It seemed to Anastasia that the Palace whirled around them and dissolved.

They were on a high mountain far above the world – a man and a woman alone – touched by the Divine.

As the King drew her closer and still closer, they were no longer two people but one and she thought it was impossible to feel the rapture and ecstasy that seeped through her, and not die of the wonder of it.

Finally, he raised his head to look down at her shining eyes, her flushed cheeks and the softness of her lips.

"You are lovely!" he said unsteadily, "so incredibly, unbelievably lovely! Am I dreaming this, or is it true?"

"It is – true."

"And you love me?"

"You – know I do."

"With your mind as well as with your body?"

"With – all of me. There is – nothing that is not – yours!"

*

Very much later Anastasia stirred against the King's shoulder.

The mother-of-pearl shell over their heads glowed in the moonlight shining through the open windows.

"Are you – happy?" she asked in a whisper.

"I did not know such happiness existed," he answered. "But there is a question, my darling, I want to ask you."

"What is – it?"

"Did you, my sweet, touch the stars?"

"I thought we were – both a part of – them."

"And did I take you down into the very depths of the sea?"

"You know – you did," she replied. "But *'making love'* was more wonderful – more – glorious than either of those things."

She gave a deep sigh and hid her face and then she said,

"I can hear the nightingales."

"It is my heart singing," the King replied.

"I – wanted so much to be – here with – you."

"It is a Palace for lovers – we will live here in the spring and summer and only go to Sergei in the winter."

"How – wonderful! Wonderful!"

"That is what you want?"

"Oh, I do – because I feel it is enchanted, like the Palace of the *Sleeping Beauty*."

The King pulled her closer and her body was very soft against his.

"And now the *Sleeping Beauty* is awake! Did I ever believe that English women were cold?"

"You are not – shocked that I should – love you so – much and that you – excite me?" Anastasia asked.

After a moment the King kissed her hair.

"Are you thinking of what your mother said to you?"

"Y-yes."

"Forget it – nothing we could ever do together would be shocking, my precious, for the fire of love which consumes us both is sanctified, as you told me it would be. We love each other not only with our bodies but with our minds."

"It is difficult to know where one – ends and the other – begins."

The King smiled very tenderly.

"There is no division when one is in love, as I am in love with you and, my perfect darling, like you, this has never happened to me before."

"Is that true – really true?" Anastasia asked.

"I swear I had no idea that love could be so ecstatic, so utterly and completely perfect."

"You will – teach me, so that you will not grow – bored with – me?" Anastasia asked.

"I shall never do that," the King answered, "not only because you are the most entrancing, adorable and desirable woman in the whole world and your beauty staggers me whenever I look at you, but also because your mind has already stimulated and, as I have told you, inspired me."

His lips were against her forehead as he went on,

"I cannot do all I want to do without your help, Anastasia. That is something I never expected to say to any woman, but I am saying it to you because it is the truth. I not only want you, I need you."

He paused for a moment and then he added in a deep voice,

"I knew when you held me in your arms in the cave and I put my face against your breast that you were not only my wife but also my mother, and at the same time a child that I must teach. You are everything I ever longed for – the ideal woman a man dreams of but never expects to find."

He kissed her eyes before he said,

"I love you, I desire you, my wonderful wife, and I worship you!"

Anastasia felt the tears come into her eyes at his touch and the wonder of what he was saying to her.

She put up her arm to draw his head down to hers and once again his lips took possession of her.

She felt her whole body quiver against him and he was carrying her up towards the stars and down into the depths of the sea.

In mind and body, heart and soul, they merged together and became one.

OTHER BOOKS IN THIS SERIES

The Barbara Cartland Eternal Collection is the unique opportunity to collect all five hundred of the timeless beautiful romantic novels written by the world's most celebrated and enduring romantic author.

Named the Eternal Collection because Barbara's inspiring stories of pure love, just the same as love itself, the books will be published on the internet at the rate of four titles per month until all five hundred are available.

The Eternal Collection, classic pure romance available worldwide for all time.

Made in the USA
Las Vegas, NV
21 November 2024

12314044R00146